James E. T. Rogers

The British Citizen

his rights and privileges - A short history

James E. T. Rogers

The British Citizen
his rights and privileges - A short history

ISBN/EAN: 9783337406226

Printed in Europe, USA, Canada, Australia, Japan

Cover: Foto ©Andreas Hilbeck / pixelio.de

More available books at **www.hansebooks.com**

THE PEOPLE'S LIBRARY.

THE BRITISH CITIZEN:

HIS RIGHTS AND PRIVILEGES.

A SHORT HISTORY.

BY

JAMES E. THOROLD ROGERS, M.P.

PUBLISHED UNDER THE DIRECTION OF THE COMMITTEE
OF GENERAL LITERATURE AND EDUCATION APPOINTED BY THE
SOCIETY FOR PROMOTING CHRISTIAN KNOWLEDGE.

LONDON:

SOCIETY FOR PROMOTING CHRISTIAN KNOWLEDGE,
NORTHUMBERLAND AVENUE, CHARING CROSS, W.C.;

43, QUEEN VICTORIA STREET, E.C.;
26, ST. GEORGE'S PLACE, HYDE PARK CORNER, S.W.
BRIGHTON: 135, NORTH STREET.

NEW YORK: E. & J. B. YOUNG AND CO.

1885.

CONTENTS.

4 CONTENTS.

THE BRITISH CITIZEN:

HIS RIGHTS AND PRIVILEGES.

————◦:◦————

CHAPTER I.

INTRODUCTION.

I T is my purpose in this little work to point out to my readers how it has been that the modern Englishman has, in the course of ages, attained his present place as a citizen, with the rights and privileges which belong to that condition. The story is not a continuous one, for the Englishman has occupied at different periods a position of very different strength or security. But his condition has been progressive, for, with very rare exceptions, the reverses of one period have not been disasters. The social progress of the English people has never run the risk, we may almost say incurred the certainty, of that downfall which visited those homes of ancient civilization, the sites of which are some of the fairest treasures of literature and art, the ruins of which are perpetual objects of interest, of curiosity, of admiration, and above all of warning. We now know that far back in time there was amazing civilization and wealth in Egypt, in the plains of Mesopotamia, in the tableland of the upper Tigris, in Persia, and along the shores of the Black Sea. Asia Minor was full of opulent cities. The southern shores of the Mediterranean were populous and wealthy; Tyre and Carthage pushed their commerce through a canal to the Red Sea and, it is said, even round Africa. But all or nearly all those sites of ancient civilization are now desolate, and the waste places of the earth are now to be found where its gardens blossomed and bore fruit aforetime.

But this reverse which came on ancient civilization is not the only noteworthy phenomenon in the history of the human race. England was by no means the first European country which started on the race of progress. Our country had hardly the beginning of a literature when the most perfect compositions in the Italian language were published and copied. It borrowed the elements of its manufactures from neighbours who were far more advanced in the arts of life. Other countries had vigorous and apparently stable institutions when England was in the grasp of foreign conquerors, and apparently without any of the realities of national life and hope. There were parliaments older than those of England, rights recognized as the inalienable property of citizens among other communities at a time when the mass of Englishmen were reputed to be without rights. There were prosperous trading cities at a time when English sailors hardly ventured out of sight of the coast. In the darkest times of the English people's life, there were kingdoms in the far east at Bagdad, and in the far west at Grenada, where opulence was general, learning was cultivated, and everything seemed to promise a secure future.

But the early promise of these nations passed away. The genius and the free institutions of Italy had a very short duration. The manufactures of Flanders and southern France were well-nigh extirpated. The parliaments of Spain and France were silenced, and the liberties of the people were violently reft from them. The trading cities and markets of the Middle Ages, the wealth of which was the object of admiration or envy to their rude neighbours, have become desolate and deserted, and the flourishing Mohammedan kingdoms of the far east and the far west have long been subject to other lords. But even when these changes took place, England was still backward among the nations.

The sequel, however, is most remarkable. The institutions of England have been imitated by all civilized nations. The model of her parliaments has been set up in every European

community and in the New World. Representatives of the people are elected in other
countries on her systems, and debate according
to English practice or habit is customary in
them. The men who speak the English
language, who consider the English literature
their heritage, and English history their history,
are far more numerous than the inhabitants of
these islands. There seems little doubt that, at
no remote period, the English speech will be
the language of the civilized world, and even be
the means through which nations which are not
descended from our stock will partake of the
advantages which our constitution has secured
to us. It is quite worth while to search into,
and, if possible, to discover the causes of so
singular a state of things.

I do not state these facts with a view to dis-
missing other equally obvious truths. We must
not believe that the progress and the extension
of our social and political history has landed us
in anything near perfection. They who take
account of English social life, and they are
many, are painfully alive to many shortcomings
in the national character, to many grievous
deficiencies and ill practices in our public and
private life. Nations, like individuals, can claim
no immunity from error, are unable to secure
themselves invariably against wrongdoing.
But if what is said above is accurate—and no
one can dispute the fact—we have had either the
good fortune or the prudence to escape some of

the casualties and errors which have wrecked the progress of nations whose future at one time seemed to be far more assured than our own. It is assuredly, also, not vainglorious for a people to examine into the causes which have given them so singular a power of instructing other nations in the arts of government and the progress of human liberty. In the first instance, we borrowed the forms of our representative system and municipal self-government from the practices of other countries. But we have maintained, have completed, and, to the present extent of our knowledge and power, have perfected them ourselves. They are, like our laws, of our own growing, though we may have imported the seed, or even the plant. We have exported the product freely and widely.

In treating this topic it will be necessary for me to touch on the very origin of our social life, the particulars of which do not differ widely from those of other civilized nations, and to discover as best I may, from the political and social history of our people, what have been the special causes which have brought about present results. The principal cause, I think, we shall find to have been that divergent interests have been schooled into aiming at and attaining common benefits.

CHAPTER II.

THE AGRICULTURAL SETTLEMENT.

THE first stage in civilization is the agricultural settlement, with the power and the practice of self-government.   All research into the history of nations is conclusive on this point.   These settlements can be traced in the beginnings of every race which has made progress.   They are found in the remotest times throughout Hindo-stan, and they remain there to this day.   They were characteristic of those races in Greece and Italy, in Asia and Africa, which grew into the opulent and famous cities in which so much in the early history of civilization was developed. It is most probable that these settlements were made among races which were incapable of this elementary association, and who therefore gradually perished, or were taught the practices of their invaders and were slowly assimilated with them.   The early narrative, frequently of no historical exactness, but unquestionably true in outline, of all the great races which have in-fluenced the world, affirms that the race was immigrant.   The Greeks said that they came from Asia, the Romans claimed a similar origin. The Israelites settled on land which they wrested, in part at least, from an earlier popu-lation, or appropriated because it had not been

settled or cultivated. The English people have
made conquests as other European nations
have, but they are the only people in modern
Europe who have colonized as these ancient
peoples did. Such colonies, and such colonies
only, grow into nations. The English colonies
in North America, including the United States,
in Australasia, and partially elsewhere, are cases
in point. These parts of the world have been
occupied in modern times, the difference of ages
being considered, as England, and indeed Scotland on the south and east, were occupied after
the fall of the Roman empire.

The Romans had occupied England as the
English have occupied India. They had garri-
sons in it, cities in it, villas in it. They raised
armies from its inhabitants, as the Indian government does from the native races. But they
never, as in what is modern France, and was
anciently called Gaul, became one with the
people. Had they done so, the basis of the
English language, like that of the French language, would have been Latin. As it was, in
all likelihood, the mass of the older inhabitants
of Great Britain, during the four centuries in
which the Romans were here, were entirely un-
affected by the presence of their masters. They
were kept from marauding by the presence of
the army and the government, and, when army
and government were gone, there was nothing
to resist a foreign invader, except perhaps the
inhabitants of a few towns, who were able

throughout to hold their own.   Such towns
were London, Winchester, York, and Exeter.
The continued existence of such places had a
potent influence in the future of England.

Long before Rome quitted Britain she had to
ward off as best she could those settlers from
the north who strove to land in this country.
When she was gone, the only hindrances to the
settlement were the Romanized inhabitants of
the towns.   Many of these held their own, and
were not dispossessed.   Some were destroyed ;
never, I imagine, unless they resisted the invaders, who wished to settle not in towns, but
on agricultural land.   The new-comers had less
civilization than the old rulers, but much more
than the mass of the native inhabitants, who in
all likelihood had only partially learned to prac-
tise agriculture at all, and were probably the
savage tribes who, when Roman domination
was at an end, rose up against their Romanized
fellow-countrymen.   The rising of the subdued
Britons is, I have no doubt, the true story of
Hengist, of Horsa, of Rowena and Vortigern,
of the Picts and the Saxons.

However it was that they made good their
footing, it is certain that the invaders did so, and
established themselves in their several settlements between the fifth and seventh centuries.
These settlements have survived to our own
time in the form of parishes.   I do not mean
to say that the parishes of to-day are the same
in number and the same in extent as they were

from twelve to fourteen centuries ago, between which periods most of England was planted and named. But thousands of our modern parishes represent the settlements of that new race which was called by many names—some names of origin or race, some of relative geographical position. At last, as seems from accident, the settlers gave this country the name of England, after one of the tribes which contributed to the settlement.

The settlers created the parish. This social unity or corporation has been known by many names at various periods of its history. The two names which have survived the longest are manor and parish. But these words are long subsequent to the formation of that which they designate, and refer to changes which came over them in the course of centuries, for the one is indicative of the Norman conquest, the other of an ecclesiastical organization. The new-comers had a religion, in which the powers of nature appear to have been worshipped, but under forms which lent themselves without much violence to the Christianity which was afterwards embraced. They seem to have recognized a good and evil principle, a Divine Being whose life was sacrificed by violence, the immortality of the soul, and a personal existence after death.

Even if we had no direct evidence on the subject we might be certain that these settlements were of the same character as those which were described, perhaps with some amplifications, centuries before, and as those which are still to be discovered now. The essence of the system was seclusion or separation from any other settlement, and self-government. It was entirely self-contained. All the inhabitants were reputed to be descended from a common ancestor, and they did not admit strangers among them. Every one had land. The whole community had common pasture and common wood, the former for feeding their cattle, the latter for fuel and building their houses. They built their huts pretty close together, generally on the sides of those ancient roads which the Romans had made. The wood was the first boundary of the settlement. Beyond it was a waste, a no-man's land. The boundaries of the settlement were guarded with jealousy, and it was a high crime to disturb them. There is no doubt that in many country places villagers' cottages occupy the same site which they occupied when the first settlers dwelt on them, just as there are places where nearly the same speech is spoken as was uttered there so long ago.

Every government, even of the smallest community, must undertake two duties. It must regulate the rights of property, and it must protect persons from fraud and violence. It probably invests some person with the authority which is necessary for carrying out the decisions of the community, whether they be on civil or criminal cases; *i.e.* it constitutes a head man of

the village.   But the action of such a person is
limited to presiding over the assembly of the
settlement, and to executing, either in person or
by command, the decree which he is bidden to
pronounce.

It is almost certain that from the beginning
individuals possessed private property in land.
Had it been always held in common, it is difficult to see how private ownership could have
been developed.   The Irish villages held arable
land in common, and it required the energetic
action of a foreign power to extinguish the
custom, and even under these circumstances it
was extinguished very slowly.   But though land
was so much distributed, the risks of life were
so serious that it is probable that population
progressed very slowly, and that the number of
families suffered scarcely any change.

The property which each person possessed in
the ploughed field of the parish was that of a
certain number of strips, bounded by a narrow
ridge of unploughed ground from that of his
neighbour.   To this ownership the son, on the
death of his father, was admitted in view of the
whole villagers, and by some symbol, as a clod
or a twig being delivered to him.   In this manner
there was public evidence of his property.   There
are ancient legal customs in England, from which
it appears that if a man married a woman from
another settlement, her relations could acquire
no rights in the place of her adoption.

There were of course offences and offenders

in these settlements. When wrongs were committed, the offender was brought before the head man and his offence was certified, before the head man could take any action. If it was proved that he had committed the deed, he was fined, all crimes being punished by this process, even homicide. We possess the codes of many Teutonic races, and from an early date. In all these the principal part of the code is the assessment of fines, which differ, first according to the extent of the injury, next according to the dignity of the injured person. The fine went to the injured person. If the offender could not or would not pay, he became the slave of the person he had wronged, and, in case he had slain a man, of his representative. In all likelihood, too, the debtor who could not meet his obligations was made the slave of his creditor. In this way many persons were reduced to the condition of servitude from early times. Some became the absolute bondsmen of their creditors, some suffered a partial bondage, *i.e.* had to work for a specified time.

The vestry of a parish, it has been observed, is the most ancient of English institutions. It represents the old gatherings of the primæval settlement. The parson of the parish presides as the head man of the village did of yore. The parson is admitted to his office by symbols which represent the ancient method by which every freeholder was recognized, for he is handed the key of the church, and takes bodily possession

of the edifice. It is true that other arrange-
ments have been made for the admission of lay
persons to their tenements, and for the chastise-
ment of offenders ; but the old customs remained
very long, and, when writing became general,
they were transcribed in thousands of documents
which still survive.

CHAPTER III.

THE RACE KINGDOMS.

THE settlement, then, is complete in itself—is
exactly like the state in little. No stranger
has rights within it, and it has no rights over its
neighbours. The jealousy of neighbouring
villages is still discernible in many places. At
the same time, there must have been some
intercourse for primitive trade or barter. Such
intercourse was held at stated times, outside the
boundary of the village and on neutral ground.
This was the origin of the fair. When in the
course of time cities were frequented, the same
rule of fixed days prevailed. But as the city or
town preserved a special form of self-government
or in time procured it, the trading was done
within the town. This was the origin of the
market.

This isolated organization could not last without the establishment of another organization.
It is most likely that from the very beginning

these villages were enrolled under some one chieftain or superior. All the settlements of which we read occupied the country under a leader. The invaders won a battle over the natives, made their settlements, and then pushed on. There were common interests and common duties. Even when the country seemed conquered, the settlers were liable to sudden incursions from their old foes. The leader, too, had to be maintained, to have his portion assigned to him and his family, in larger measure than the other invaders had. There was plenty of room for him and his. It seems that nearly all our present shires were originally little kingdoms, for we find names of kings whose dominions and even whose existence are not recorded in written history.

Very speedily these kings gathered round themselves followers whom they kept near them and rewarded with grants of land. The power of the king kept constantly growing, especially in comparison with that of the little agricultural settlements, who could be employed for a common purpose only under some leader. He therefore claimed the attendance of the male population in war for the defence of the whole race, and in order to make his summons effective divided his dominions into certain parcels. He did not meddle with the jurisdiction of the settlement, but those who were under his authority were made liable, at least for certain purposes, to another law, that of the king, and to other magistrates than those of their own little local court. The king, too, had a far wider authority over his own immediate followers, who began to take higher rank than the village settlers did, though they were only called the king's servants.

After a time the different kingdoms began to make war on each other. They had driven the natives away, or thoroughly vanquished them, and they now sought to aggrandize themselves on the people of their own race. When history begins to be written about them only a few of these petty kingdoms survive, and at last one achieves a nominal and uncertain supremacy over the rest. By this time the king is attended by a body of nobles, still under the old names, who have become opulent and powerful.

Now, however, there is a new danger at hand (about 780). The invaders are invaded in their turn, and the kingdom which seemed to be founded on the conquest of the whole country, is made to suffer the direst reverses. The east side of England, always in early times the most populous and fertile, is occupied by the new-comers. These, however, in time, though not without fierce and cruel struggles, settle down peacefully by the side of their old foes. There never was a country so often conquered within a few centuries as England was during the first six hundred years of the so-called Saxon period. After the last of these conquests its continuous public history begins, and with this its progress.

Less than two centuries after the first settlement (602), Christianity was preached in England, and made slow and very fitful progress, for much of England remained fiercely pagan long after the first missionaries came. They brought with them from Italy the system of government by bishops, which, though general in the Christian world, does not seem to have been universal, and appears to have been far from being developed in these islands, for though an English bishop is named before the Saxon conquest, we do not hear that a see was assigned to him. The bishop rapidly became the second person in the state ; and probably when the oldest sees were founded, there were as many kings as there were bishops. The see was generally fixed in some obscure or small hamlet, where there was convenience for the bishop and his missionary monks. Some of them, however, were placed in the old Roman towns ; as, for example, at London, Winchester, and Canterbury.

Now, it was inevitable that, in the midst of such incessant war and such perpetual disasters, many persons should be reduced from a free condition to one of servitude. In the early history of all nations, the vanquished warrior, if his life is spared, becomes the slave of the victor. The losses of a surprise in one of the settlements would disable a debtor from paying his debts. He became a slave. Or he committed some offence, and could not pay the heavy penalty laid on him ; for as the power of the king and his authority grew, the fines for misconduct were multiplied and enlarged.   The king's nobles or servants received large grants of land from their master, and wanted slaves to inhabit and culti-vate them.   The slave must live, so he was provided with land, sufficient, after he had worked for his lord, to maintain himself and his family.   Unless the lord emancipated him, he could not by any effort of his own rise above his calling, or raise his children above it.   Hence the class of serfs was always increasing at the expense or loss of the free inhabitants.   It is possible that there were personal slaves, *i.e.* slaves who were not settled on land and engaged in agriculture, but who constituted the household of their lord.   But it is not very likely.   Among all the Teutonic nations domestic service was honourable.   The proudest nobles did not dis-dain to do what we should call menial service to the king.   We see it in the king's chamber-lain, *i.e.* his personal attendant; his marshal, which really means his chief groom of the stables, his butler, his steward, and the controller of his household; and what the kings did with their closest personal associates, the noble did with his.

There was, however, still another change to come.   We have left the freeholders greatly diminished in numbers and weakened, but still tenaciously holding to their settlement and its usages.   The lord in the neighbourhood enters into a bargain with them.   The king is his over-

lord, he will be their overlord under the king,
to whom they already owe substantial duties.
In return for the place he gets, he will defend
them.   They must turn their border woodland
into his forest, where they will have rights of
fuel and timber, but he has the soil.   He will
secure them their local jurisdiction.   All great
injuries shall be fined as before, and go to the
injured party ; all fines for smaller breaches of
the peace, and the proceeds of other police
matters, shall go to him, and be assessed by his
representatives.   He will not preside over the
court himself, and his steward shall not be able
to punish a single offender, unless the inhabitants
inform against him.   In this way he cannot
oppress them, for if his steward is rapacious, he
will get no fines, and the steward will not, on
the other hand, lend himself to party spite.   So
far, he is offering them a real service and pre-
serving their liberties.   He is, however, going
to do more—to defend them everywhere and
against all.   If they choose to fight with him,
he will take the service for a limited time, and
will only call on them to help and aid him as he
aids the king.   If they do not wish to fight,
except at the king's summons, to which they
are already liable, and which they dare not disobey, he will protect them, and most likely get
them off the risk.   Let them pay him a rent for
their holding, and he will secure them from all
but the king's claims.

I don't think an Anglo-Saxon farmer, when

the Danes were about, could refuse this bargain. To be sure, he had to hold from a man what before he had held from God and by his own right hand only. But the thane was rich and strong, and he was weak. He fell into the bargain, perhaps he was forced to accept it; and thus began what is called the feudal system.

CHAPTER IV.

THE GROWTH OF THE KING'S POWER.

THE freeholder in the old sense of the word, that is, the freeman who had a holding in the soil, and who owed nothing to any man, unless it were the obligation to drive out an invading enemy in concert with his fellows, had entered into a new obligation at last, to an overlord. In other countries, where the original population had not been extirpated or driven away, it is more than probable that this relation of lord and vassal had been developed in very early times. In England it was a supremacy of Englishmen over Englishmen, and must have seemed at first harsh and unnatural. But, as I have said, the right of village self-government in the tenure of property and the protection of persons was secured to the inhabitants, and therefore the change of the new system may not have been very irritating.

Loyalty as yet was, as far as these people

went, confined to the respect which such persons had to their local customs and their local authorities. In one particular, the village was merciless. It considered that treason to the settlement was the most unpardonable of offences. The collections of the old German customs, from which our own are undoubtedly derived, show that the most frightful punishments were inflicted on those who committed treason against the collective settlement. These punishments were ultimately incorporated into the horrible law of treason, which prevailed in England for four centuries or more.

Whether the allegiance to the king preceded that to the overlord or followed it cannot be made out. As the king's servants were to him, so were the lord's dependants to the lord. The dependence of the inferior husbandman on his superior was undoubtedly borrowed in form from the dependence of the king's servants on their own master. But that the king should claim the allegiance of his whole people was natural. It was, first, a condition of the public defence. There were in those days no standing armies. The national force was of the king's dependants and the rural militia. Next, the authority of the king grew naturally. He was from the beginning the principal person in the nation or race or tribe. His office was limited to the members of one family, from which the most suitable was chosen. It was inevitable that his authority should increase. Next, he was the accepted leader in war, and war was the customary condition of the times—war against neighbouring kingdoms, war against foreign invaders. It was impossible for such a people to have lasting peace. They must all be ready for war, and for a war under a natural and tried leader. Every parish had, no doubt, its strong place, its stockade, to which the people could fly and carry their goods and cattle from marauders ; but the battle was fought in the open country.

The king therefore claimed the allegiance of all his subjects. As far as we can find, this was claimed formally only a generation or two before the Norman conquest. For a long time, the only legal protection of the king was the large fine which was exacted from any offender who did him a personal injury or took his life. But even this was an extension of the custom of the village to a custom in the kingdom.

There can be no doubt that the authority of the prince was greatly aided by the conversion of the English to Christianity. The bishop of the Saxon England was almost always a statesman as well as an ecclesiastic. He was the principal person at the royal court. But he was also the centre of ecclesiastical government, and a government which was very central. From tradition, or policy, or convenience, the bishop was the chief of a body of monks. The establishment of the parochial clergy was later in England than that of the monasteries, and the monks roaming about the country were the agents by which the pagan English were brought over to Christianity. But an institution which had so exceedingly centralized a system, was an obvious and a convenient means for enforcing deference to the central secular ruler. The king had every reason for employing the services and for listening to the counsels of the bishop.

Still, the whole country, even at the best of times, had but a very slight cohesion. It was constantly exposed to invasion. At intervals for a century and a half, it struggled with the Danes, who at last succeeded in planting a dynasty of their own kings on the throne. The succession was changed again, and a new order of things with an entirely new departure began with the Conquest. The progress, continuous but unequal, of the later Englishman commences with this epoch.

I have, however, prepared this sketch of the social condition of England in these remote times, because so much of the old life remains at the present time. The church of the parish occupied at once the place where the elders of the village met, where the old religion was practised, and where the stronghold of the village was surrounded by a stockade. The tower of the church was often, very often, the castle of the villagers, and the body of the church was the outwork of that last defence. Here they stored in times of danger their most precious possessions. One of the most characteristic cities of the later Saxon epoch is Oxford.

It grew up under one or two Saxon monasteries, which were planted on a site which was naturally a stronghold. The daughter of the great Alfred raised a mound here of considerable height, which, as the manner of their fortification was, she certainly crowned with a strong stockade. This was at the most defensible part of the area enclosed in the town. At the north and the south stood two churches, each dedicated to the archangel Michael. These were watch towers, erected before the walls, from which the inhabitants might espy the approaching enemy—in which, as in other defended places, they might take refuge and attack the invaders.

Englishmen, though they have happily attained, under what would seem to have been great obstacles, that genuine love of country which makes them act with a common purpose, and yet with that local feeling which makes them cherish local associations, cling greatly to the past. I believe that the great majority of us are convinced that the county of our birth is the best part of England, and if we were born countryfolk, that our parish or village of the county is the most favoured spot in it. The sentiment is not growing weaker. The English people has had to struggle against the attempts of government (very natural attempts, for the administration of all human affairs aims at doing its work in the most methodical and easy way) to constrain local feeling into acquiescence with central government, and after a struggle for

ages has effected a compromise.   It is beginning
to understand what that government should do,
and it is gradually striving, and will in the end
succeed in formulating, what a central government should not do, but should leave to local
institutions.

There is hardly an effort made after social
reform, which does not, perhaps unconsciously,
seek to revive the institutions of our remote
forefathers.   There is an active party which
seeks to give the inhabitants of every parish a
direct and immediate control over all houses of
entertainment.   It is merely striving to revive
what was done for centuries by the senate of the
mediæval village.   There are a good many
persons who think that the local magistrate
should be elected by the suffrages of his fellows.
To do so would be to revive early usage.   If
the elders of the village presented to such a
local authority such offenders as have created
scandal and inflicted minor injuries on their
neighbours, they would revive the old jury of
the court leet, and perhaps be more effectual in
maintaining a just order than the local policeman
and the justice's parlour can.   For the essence
of the ancient village was self-government, and
now that national unity is an inveterate sentiment in Englishmen's minds, the completion of
the system is the restoration of local self-government.   I can conceive nothing which would aid
habits of thrift and order more than that experience which our forefathers had, and the wisest

of philosophers enunciated, that the best social education of men is that under which they learn how to be ruled wisely, and how to rule wisely. In his youth, the villager was under the authority of his elders, not indeed of his father only, but of the senators of the settlement ; in his age, he became one of the local parliament himself. He might, as time went on, even though he bore by birth the ineffaceable mark of serfdom, be the head man of the village, the trusted depositary of the lord's confidence, of his business and his favours. The process by which he was turned from a villager, whose whole experiences and hopes were centred in the place of his birth, whose conceptions of the world outside him were shadowy and undefined, and who could not be expected to realize any rights or duties which lay outside his little world, into an English citizen with a love of country has to be described. It was a very slow process ; it can scarcely be said to be completed yet, for it takes some time after public rights are recognized, before these rights are interpreted under the rule of public duties.

CHAPTER V.

ENGLAND AT THE CONQUEST.

At the time of the Conquest (1066) there were three strong forces in England, whose interests might be harmonized, but which were constantly

at variance, as they remained from time to time
at variance for centuries.   These were the king,
who represented the central authority ; the
Church, which guided the religious and in some
degree the social progress of the people, and
had now begun to be divided into the *regular*
clergy, by which is meant the monks ; and the
secular, by which is meant the parochial, clergy.
The monasteries affected to be independent of
the bishop's authority, and to be under the direct
control of the Roman Church, though, for reasons
which I shall give further on, this control was
not very effective.

The English Church was the result of a
missionary effort from Rome itself.   The conversion spread rapidly in the south and the
east, but was for a long time resisted in the
great midland kingdom of Mercia.   At last this
part of England yielded, and the zeal of the
Saxon missionaries from England was as great
and more courageous than that of Augustine
and his companions, for it was an Englishman
(Wilfrid, known afterwards as St. Boniface) who
was the apostle of Germany.   For a time the
bishops were Italians.   Once a Greek of Tarsus
sat at Canterbury.   But very soon the bishops
were English, and the Church became entirely
national.   In truth, for some time before the
Norman conquest, the Roman Church was in
extreme weakness and discredit, till at last,
almost at the crisis of the Conquest, a great
internal reform in its discipline and conduct was
effected.

The nobles had been, it seems, originally the descendants of those royal houses which had finally been constrained to submit to the single king of England. In course of time there were aldermen in nearly every county. Besides these there were the king's thanes or servants, who now had become the overlords of the peasantry, and into whose ranks men with a certain amount of fortune would be ranged. The principal officers of the king were the alderman, the bishop, and the sheriff—the first concerned with the civil government of the country, the second with its religion as well as with a great amount of secular business, the third with the king's revenue, which was derived from the numerous estates belonging to the king, his dues as over-lord, and his claims to extraordinary aid. This it was the sheriff's business to collect. In the latest epoch of the Saxon kingdom the principal part of the administration was in the hands of a few great earls, who seem to have been appointed by the king and to be responsible to him. The name "earl" was derived from the Danes.

William the Norman claimed to be the heir of the Saxon monarchs, and to succeed to the amplest rights which they had enjoyed. He was at once, therefore, by the act of conquest, the heir to all the royal estates, and also the heir by forfeiture to all which had been possessed by Harold and his brothers. The battle in which he won the crown had further enriched him by the forfeiture of many of those who had taken Harold's side ; and as he had to provide for his followers as well as to strengthen himself, his first victory was followed by extensive forfeitures. The dispossessed English nobles rebelled, and were subdued. At last, and towards the conclusion of his reign, when Domesday was compiled, almost all the old Saxon thanes were dispossessed, and Normans were put in their room.

Beyond securing his own authority and rewarding his successors, William had no wish to change the constitution of the country, least of all to interfere with the local customs and self-government of the villages. The inhabitants of these places exchanged a Saxon overlord for a Norman overlord, and very likely did not find the latter more oppressive than the former had been. Even during the disorders of Stephen's reign (1135–1154), though the new system of building stone castles gave at once the means of licence and the means of refuge to the oppressor, there is no reason to believe that the peasant suffered more than he did during the wars of the rival Saxon kingdoms and the incursions of the Danes. When we come across contemporary evidence of his condition, we find him in possession of local self-government, as we know he must have been in possession of it during the ages of the first English settlement. It could not have been destroyed and revived ; it must have been continuous and unbroken.

The Roman Church had reformed itself, and the Papacy, which had been a generation or two before an object of contempt, was now occupying a most conspicuous and powerful position in Western Europe. The new king determined on reforming and recasting the English Church. He knew that with their great political influence, English bishops and English abbots might, and probably would, harbour and encourage disaffection towards the new dynasty. So on various pretexts they were dispossessed, as the English nobles were, and their places were filled with Normans. But William would not allow his bishops to be dependent on the Pope, or to be his creatures. They were to be his men first, and the Pope's men after him. Very speedily they showed themselves to be on the side of public liberty, at least against misgovernment. In time the best of them gave their influence on behalf of the English people as against the Norman ruler. But for nearly a century after the Conquest, the chiefs of the English Church were foreigners. The first person of English descent who was raised to dignity in the Church, is said to have been Becket.

But, as may well be imagined, the Saxon nobles did not submit quietly to dispossession. They became outlaws, they revolted, they made war on the new king. They were put down, dispersed, hunted. They took to the desperate remedy of assassinating the Normans, and left no trace of their identity. The king upon this sent his own judges whenever a murdered Norman was found, and called upon the hundred to produce the culprit. If they failed to do this, they were fined in what was a large sum for the time. The outlaws then strove to destroy the evidence of their victim's origin. The king met this by enacting that any murdered person was to be taken to be a Norman, and that the proof of who the murderers were must be supplied, unless it could be shown it was an Englishman.

Now, these offences we may be certain were not committed in the villages, but outside their boundaries, in the forest, in the unoccupied districts. If the villagers had done such a deed, they would have concealed the evidence of it, if they were strong enough, and would have been punished in their local courts if they were not. Besides, it was a fundamental law of the settlement that no stranger should be harboured there. If a villager had a guest, he must give notice to the authorities. If he harboured one, he must be responsible for his conduct. If a stranger was a guest beyond a given time, generally three days, the host was not only liable for his acts, but was fined. The enactment of William, then, though intended for the protection of his followers and his officials, put on villages collectively the obligation of keeping the peace and maintaining order beyond the boundaries of their own settlements.

The inquiry was made by a jury, who were *witnesses* to the fact. It was the essence of early

English society that every man should know about the conduct of his neighbour, and should be cognizant of his actions. Such a discipline could be of no injury to an honest man, and must be of great strength to society, because it nips misdoings in the bud. There still remain quaint relics in country villages of the old custom and duty, where personal misconduct is visited with rough music and rough justice.

The jury system is older than Alfred, and younger than Alfred. It is older, because the villager from the first sat in judgment on offenders, who were always liable to be tried by their peers, as they were liable before the English people emigrated from the forests of Germany. It is younger, because the obligation of juries being witnesses of the fact, when the offence was committed beyond the boundaries of the settlement, dates from a time after the Norman conquest. It was still later, for it was not till the reign of Charles II., that a jury was declared to be irresponsible for the verdict which it gave, and was not rendered liable to punishment for refusing to accept the judge's law, or the crown's desires; for there were very often strong reasons which led the crown to press for a conviction by fair means or foul, and for judges to do all in their power, for even more substantial reasons, in order to further these desires.

The indirect consequences of William's action were far more important. It put the duty of inquiring into the gravest offences, those of murder, on the central authority, and gradually took it from the local court. It is true that, if an offender was taken in the act, he could be punished by the local authorities. The last case which I have found in which capital punishment is inflicted in a parish court, is in 1337, nearly three centuries after the Conquest. In this case the culprit had stolen an outer garment in a public-house, had run away with it, had been followed by hue and cry, had been captured, and was taken with the article in his possession. He was forthwith tried by a jury, found to be a vagabond, to have no property, and was adjudged to be hanged, the sentence being forthwith executed. The case, it will be seen, shows how harshly the local jury would treat a stranger who committed an offence, and that it was well, at least, to take so great a power out of hands which might use it with such excessive severity. An inhabitant of the village would have been visited with a moderate fine only, perhaps treated as a practical joker.

Now, however, in this one crime the duty of investigating into and punishing the offence was put on the king's judges, who might be supposed to be interested in nothing more than keeping the peace and punishing offenders. In course of time the jurisdiction extended to all capital offences, and to some which were not capital, and the authority of the local court fell to something less than that exercised by magistrates and at petty sessions.

In other countries, however, the higher jurisdiction remained in local courts and under the
control of local authorities, which became almost
absolute till late times, and the power was
atrociously abused. In Scotland they who
possessed heritable jurisdiction had the right of
inflicting capital punishment within their own
domain till 1746. In France it lasted till 1789,
and the abuses of the system led in no small
degree to the frightful excesses which occurred
after the leaders of the Revolution became at
once frightened and bloodthirsty. We were
saved from these consequences at a very early
date ; and in theory, at least, the constitution
taught men that there was one law for rich and
poor alike, when an offence had been committed.

It is curious that while the writers of this
time speak of the hard usage with which the
Conqueror, his followers and successors, treated
the English, they also comment on the justice
which they caused to be administered, and on
the security which they brought about. Now,
these writers did not publish their books. They
composed them for the study of their successors
in the monasteries, and with a view to creating
an unbroken and continuous succession of
chronicles. The complaints refer to the old
Saxon aristocracy. The praise refers to the
relations of the government towards the people.

CHAPTER VI.

THE EXCHEQUER, AND THE SOCIAL STATE IT DEALT WITH.

THE Norman king, however, devised another engine of government, which has had most important and enduring effects on the social life of England.   It consisted in what is known as the Exchequer, the system of which was said to have been invented or imported by William, to have been continued by his son, and to have been revived by his great grandson.   It speedily became the centre of the administration.   Its primary object was to assure the king's revenue. But it had incidentally great and lasting effects, for out of it were developed the English Constitution, Parliamentary Government, and in the end private and public liberty.

The beginning and the purpose of the Exchequer was that of the establishment, on a permanent and exact footing, of an audit, under every condition of precision and publicity, in which the rights and dues of the king should be registered, received, receipted, and vouched. The beginning of the system was Domesday Book, which was for the greater part of England a minute survey and register of the rights of king and subject.   We do not know when this system of annual account keeping began.   We

know that it was in full operation forty years
after the Conquest, that it was suspended during
the troubles of the fourth Norman King Stephen,
and restored by his successor.   At any rate, the
earliest accounts are lost, but from the earliest
years of Henry II. (1154) down to the reign of
William IV., they exist.   No other country has
anything like them.

It is from the indirect effects of this system
that the great results alluded to above have
sprung.   To understand this, let us see what
was the state of society with which the Exchequer
had to deal.

Speaking generally, the king was the largest
landowner in the whole kingdom.   He inherited
by the Conquest the ancient estates of the
Anglo-Saxon kings, and the forfeitures of his
rival and his rival's family.   For many a generation these lands were specially characterized,
and the inhabitants in them had many privileges, as dwellers on the conqueror's domain, or
on the king's ancient domain.   Then there were
the estates of his followers, sometimes very
large, but always very scattered, for though
William rewarded his inherents generously, he
was always on his guard against them, and with
good reason, and while he wished from motives
of policy to make them powerful against the dis-
affected English, he wished also to make them
as powerless as possible against himself.   He
had really more trouble with them than he had
with the English, for by the middle of his great

grandson's reign, nearly all the great nobles of
the Conquest had been rooted out. His plan
was to scatter their estates as much as possible,
so as to prevent them from having a coherent
body of followers.

These nobles in their turn granted estates to
their dependants—a parish as it was called in
Church matters, a manor as it was known in
the secular business of life. In these manors,
the lord, who probably, indeed generally, held
of some other superior lord, granted in the same
way land to his dependants, and so every one
but the king held of some superior. No one,
except the king, held landed property absolutely.

The people who held of the king owed him
dues. These were fixed, *i.e.* payable yearly;
or casual, *i.e.* payable when some event happened in the king's family, or in the family of
the tenant. Similarly the under tenant of a
lord owed him dues, and in the same manner.
His tenants were in the same relation to their
superior. It is surprising, when one reads old
accounts, to see how large a number of rights
might be created in every parish or manor.

The special peculiarity of the system was that
all these liabilities were fixed in amount. No
one imagined, when a particular sum was set
down as the king's due, or the lord's due, that
this sum might in course of time be very inadequate in value to what it was when the
charge was first imposed and the bargain was
first made. People thought that the value of

money was the one immutable thing, and they thought so with some reason. As far as we can make out, there had been no great change in prices for five hundred years before the Conquest, and there certainly was no great change in prices for five hundred years after the Conquest. The subject then knew what were his regular liabilities to the king, and the tenant knew in just the same way and for the same reasons what were his liabilities to his lord.

All this was put down in black and white. It is true that the lords of manors and parishes did not begin to keep these registers as soon as the king did, or at least they have not been so well preserved. But there was not at first the same necessity. That which needed to be recorded in the vast estate of the crown was kept well in memory by the standing jury of the parish or manor.

The towns were generally part of the king's domain. In these there was a regular annual rent paid. In most cases, this rent was enlarged and rendered permanent by the grant of self-government—the self-government, or municipal system of the towns, being long subsequent to the self-government of the parish, manor, or commune, and probably imitated from it, with the grant of a special privilege, that of electing their own magistrates, which was occasionally the characteristic of a manor.

The only persons who had to pay nothing were the clergy. They were supposed to hold their lands free from all due, and to owe only their prayers. We shall see how, in course of time, this exemption led to certain distinct results, and that as they paid nothing regularly, they were called on to pay a great deal occasionally.

The social orders in the state were either lay or spiritual. The latter were either monks, called the regular clergy, who were under the government of abbots or priors, and strove, generally with success, to free themselves from the control of the bishops; or the parochial and cathedral clergy, who were called secular, and were under the direct government of the bishops. The clergy were entirely exempt from all the jurisdiction of the lay courts, and could be punished in the bishop's court only.

The lay people in the kingdom were either free or serf. There was, properly speaking, no nobility. We hear of earls and barons, but the title of the former, bestowed undoubtedly on opulent and powerful subjects, was official. A great man was Earl of Chester or Earl of Kent, because he was the king's vicegerent or official there. His title was hereditary because his office was, and it was gradually understood to be hereditary, because the tendency of the whole social system was to recognize the right of the eldest son to succeed to the estate and office of his father. A baron meant only one of the tenants of the crown. In law it meant the head of a family, and in the city of London it was applied to all the citizens.

It was the invariable custom for all the chiefs of the Teutonic races to be attended by a council. This council was to the king what the jury was to the manor—an assemblage of the freemen of the kingdom. Every one was liable to be summoned. But in practice only the most important were summoned. To be absent after the summons was issued was an offence and an affront, and was generally considered a sign of disaffection and intended revolt. Hence, if one of the king's men were bidden to come and did not, or could not come, he had to excuse himself, and to give sureties for his good behaviour, which were subsequently called proxies. This council was the origin of the Parliament, especially of the House of Lords, to which, two centuries after the Conquest, deputies from the towns and counties were summoned, first as an experiment, and thirty years afterwards regularly, these deputies or representatives sitting at first with the older assembly in the same council and chamber, and in the king's presence.

The freemen were of two kinds—those who were liable to attend their lord in his wars; and those who were exempt from that service, but had to pay a fixed rent for their holdings. The more opulent tenants were always under the former condition, and most, if not all, of the under lords. But this service was not always

due to the king.   It might be due to a subject,
and the greater landowners must have had
bodies of retainers who were bound to go to
war with him.   It was by the aid of those
retainers that the nobles of the Conquest rose
against the king, fought against him, were
beaten, and, finally, were in the main extirpated.
In England alone among feudal nations, the
king had a prior right to his subjects' allegiance,
even against his lord, but it required a strong
king to maintain that right.

The freeholders who paid rent were the
yeomen and husbandmen, and the citizens of
towns.   They could not be summoned to fight
except when the realm was actually invaded ;
but they were bound, in proportion to their
income, to provide themselves with a more or
less perfect set of arms and armour.   It is true
that many of these freemen in country places
had other callings besides husbandry.   But all,
it appears, had land, and this characteristic of
the freemen lasted very long, though it seems
likely that from very remote times the allot-
ments of free labourers were often insufficient for
their maintenance.   Thus there was always a
class of free labourers.

Besides these there were the serfs or villeins.
They are described by many names in Domesday.   They were disabled from leaving the
manor or parish.   They were not allowed to
bear arms.   They could not rise above their
condition.   If a serf wished to send his son to

school or university, to make him priest or monk, he had to get his lord's permission and, in historical times at least, to pay for it. He had to pay a fine when his daughter married. If he obtained permission to live away from the manor in a town, and to carry on a trade there, he had to pay an annual sum by way of licence.

It is said that at first he had no rights whatever against his lord, who could take his property, sell him, beat him, inflict any injury on him short of loss of life or limb, without redress or punishment. So the old law books tell us. But the actual records of the life of serfs in the manors do not confirm this view. Such records exist by thousands, and without exception they show that these serfs possessed land like the freemen, and sometimes in quite as large parcels; that they had stock and chattels, goods and money, and that they paid sums of money to their lords for the exercise of divers privileges —payments which would have been absurd had all their possessions been at the lord's mercy. It may be that the tenacious manner in which Englishmen clung for centuries to the system of fixed payments for land bargains may have had its influence in giving an inchoate emancipation to the slave of the old English time.

But he always paid in labour. The labour was so many days in the year at certain times of the year. Occasionally he received a small wage for this work, or allowances of provisions, or the right to carry a sheaf on his sickle out of the harvest field. From early days, too, he was permitted to purchase exemption from labour by giving money in lieu of labour. His lord would probably be glad to commute his labour for money. Forced labour is rarely very valuable or very trustworthy, and the oldest works on English farming inform us that the bailiff had to watch sharply after serf labour, as the workman was very apt to shirk it. So at last there grew up a system under which any liability could be redeemed with money. From this stage to freedom is not a long step.

CHAPTER VII.

THE OFFICERS OF THE EXCHEQUER.

THE Exchequer, as I have said, was established in order to look after and secure the punctual payment of the king's revenue. Till the king's debtor had paid his dues, he was not quit, or quiet, for the latter word is that which is used to denote his having discharged his liability. Nor did lapse of time relieve him. It was a maxim: No time is hindrance to the king. The debtor had to pay the king's local officer, or to attend at the king's exchequer, and tender his money. The money which was paid was weighed and assayed, and it was very perilous to tender bad money at the Exchequer. The officials of the department were always on the lookout to improve the king's revenue by any device which they could think of and sustain. They pried everywhere, claimed all they could claim, and enforced every liability to the utmost farthing. When they were satisfied they gave the debtor a tally, *i.e.* they split a hazel wand in two, and notched the two pieces equally. The debtor went off with his half, his discharge, and the other half was kept in the cellars of the Exchequer. The tallies were kept there for centuries, and when the system was abolished, and an order was given that the old tallies should be destroyed, the people who were set to burn them, burnt the old houses of parliament down in the process.

It will surprise none of my readers to learn that the officers of the Exchequer were very unpopular. Their hand was against every man, and when trouble arose, every man's hand was against them ; whenever the people rose against the government—and they rose many times in English history—their wrath was always directed first against the officers of the Exchequer. These officials were nearly always clergymen, and the life of a clergymen was supposed to be very sacred. But more than once in English history a bishop has been murdered by an infuriated mob, because he was associated with, and administered the hated exchequer. Thus they murdered Bishop Stapledon, in 1327, and Bishops De Moleyns and Aiscough, in 1450.

It may, therefore, well seem strange that what was so prying and so unpopular should have been the principal instrument by which the English citizen has secured his rights and liberties. But a little reflection will show how this has come about. In the first place, the expression, rights and dues of the crown, necessarily imply limitation. There is nothing due from a slave, because all he has, including his own person, belongs to his master. If the king might help himself as he pleased out of his subjects' pockets, and to any extent that he liked, as some of the flatterers of James I. said he could, the pretence of property would speedily vanish, to be followed soon after by the pretence of liberty. The claim of the crown, therefore, was a definite and fixed quantity, which could not be arbitrarily exceeded.

Besides, it was always considered to be an equivalent for some service rendered. The feudal system may have been oppressive, but it was founded on a theory of reciprocal justice. If the king took dues, he was bound to administer justice. If he called out his people in war, for the defence of the kingdom, he was bound to take his part in the defence. If he claimed allegiance, he was responsible to his people. If his people contributed to his state, he was understood to keep the peace, *i.e.* to protect them against marauders. In ordinary times, when the kingdom was freed from foreign dangers, all the duties of government were understood to be defrayed out of his estate, and it was as evil a thing for a king to waste his substance on favourites and in prodigal indulgence, as it was for him to be oppressive and tyrannical. And in English history, though acts of oppression on individuals have been only too common, it has always been exceedingly dangerous for oppression to cause public discontent.

Again, a regular, methodical, organized institution, even though it occasionally presses a right too far, is an enormously powerful instrument of public education. The weakness of the English nation in early times lay in the passionate attachment of the people to local institutions and practices. The boundary of each man's experiences is apt to be the boundary of his sympathies and duties. But nations want cohesion as well as parochialism, general patriotism as well as love of locality. A people should be centralized in certain things, decentralized in others. There are occasions on which one's sympathies should extend to the whole human race, to the whole of one nation; there are others when it is right that they should be limited to one's own family. In well-ordered minds, and in the greatest men, you will find at once the keenest personal affection and the widest sense of public duty—a sense of duty which may overleap every limit, and a tenderness of private duty which is incessantly watchful.

E

Many good men limit themselves to one of these functions. No great man has ever existed who was not great in both because he has been wise and earnest in both.

But it is hard indeed to be educated at once in public and private duty ; and most men must be trained, almost mechanically, in acquiescing in that which is of the highest service. Thus, however much men may differ in the mode under which they wish to effect the ends of good government, and may honestly differ, all are agreed that good government is an eminently desirable end, and that bad government is a very serious injury to society. They know that in this country the control over government, as well as the character of it, is determined by parliamentary elections, and in no other way. But in hardly any case, especially in the metropolis, do the number of those who record their votes represent more than a fairly high percentage of the electors, while a very large number of persons, to whom, we may conclude, wisdom in the administration of public affairs is an object, are too indolent or too indifferent to record their judgment. But we live at a time when knowledge is disseminated, when every opportunity is given for the free expression of opinion, and the means of communication are obvious and convenient.

The existence of a permanent class of officials, who were early recognized as being responsible for the advice they gave the king, and the action which followed on that advice, has been the origin of that doctrine, which has been very slowly developed, of responsibility of the advisers of the crown, and the irresponsibility of the crown itself. Centuries passed before the doctrine was finally settled. But the principle now fully admitted has done more to make the English constitution stable than anything else.

The English people has never been patient under oppression. It rose against the misgovernment of John (1216), and had he not died opportunely, would have deposed him. It rose against his son; and had not the first Edward been a far wiser man than his father, would have deposed him too. It deposed Edward II. (1327), Richard II. (1399), Henry VI. (1461), Charles I. (1648), and James II. (1688). However adversely these acts may be criticized, no one can doubt that, in each case, there was a widely prevalent opinion that the State was in danger from misgovernment. In every case the reputed misconduct of the king was visited by the punishment of his chief advisers. They were all officers of the Exchequer.

Even at this day, the machinery of the government is centred in that ancient institution. The head of the government is the chief officer of the Treasury—the minister who is immediately responsible for the public expenditure, and the taxation which is necessarily connected with it. The second officer of the government is the

minister whose business it is to adjust the
burden of taxation in the fairest and most
equitable way.   The heads of all other depart-
ments have to submit the charge of their part of
the public service to the Treasury or public
Exchequer first, and to the House of Commons
afterwards, which sits in judgment, a jury of
the whole nation on the action of the ministry,
and the machinery by which it is to be carried
out.

CHAPTER VIII.

THE KING'S PEACE, AND THE SUBJECT'S DUES.

IN modern times, it is said that the machinery
of parliamentary government is carried on by
the ministerial party, criticized and corrected by
the opposition.   The existing government rules,
their opponents examine into and impugn their
rule.   But this is the immediate result of the
system which the Norman kings introduced, and
the present condition of things is as much the
descendant of that ancient system as the present
queen derives her pedigree and title from Saxon
Egbert and Norman William, as the mass of
the English people are derived from the men
who were the inhabitants of England eight centuries ago.   The history of a nation is continuous.   We are what we are, because we have
inherited the customs as well as the blood of

our ancestors. These customs, though altered, defaced, or modified, have not been lost, and in many particulars would as well be restored in something like their old shape.

In those early times the two parties were, the king and his officials on the one side, the people on the other. There were particulars in which king and people agreed. It was expedient, nay necessary, that the peace should be kept; and, considering the times, the peace was kept wonderfully well. For a few years England endured, in a modified way, what the Germans and French endured for centuries—a robber aristocracy. But generally the country was too strong for them, for all classes of society were against them. The whole political education of England tended towards this result, that the peace must be kept; that the law must be obeyed by the highest as well as the lowest. The Church was as national as the State, and though the authority which all western Christendom recognized was also recognized in England, the Pope found he could never make a political party in England.

One of the reasons, and indeed the principal reason, why the peace was kept so well was, that nearly everybody, from the king to the serf, was engaged in husbandry at some time or other in the year. There were forests and waste places where wild animals, hunted by the king and his grandees, ranged. But these wild animals were not bred, only reserved for the sport of a few persons. I have read thousands of accounts, giving minute details of agriculture on cultivated land, and I have never once found a complaint that wild animals had wasted the crops. I doubt whether all the wild stags, wild cattle, and wild boars, in England six centuries ago, were as numerous as foxes in England are now.

Everybody cultivated land. Everybody went to market to buy and sell. Within a few miles of every village there was a fair once or twice a year, to which chapmen came and villagers resorted. In these fairs, always placed out of the local jurisdiction, every one was a stranger, and no one was a stranger; but they always had a vigorous police in the fair. There were highwaymen and robbers, but the trade of these people was dangerous, and retribution sharp. In the village the police of the neighbourhood was kept strictly. In the fair the police of the county was kept as strictly. It was in these fairs that public opinion, as we now call it, was developed, matured, and disseminated. Even as late as the Commonwealth the fair was the great centre of debate. In the " Pilgrim's Progress," Bunyan describes, under the name of Vanity Fair, and with intense religious feeling, the scene which he had often witnessed at Stourbridge fair, the great mart which was held a mile out of Cambridge, and was famous over the whole world.

Though these rustics then (for seven men

out of eight lived in these old times in country parishes, with all the machinery of local self-government in their hands, and in familiar use) were busy during most of the year on their own holdings, they went for thirty days, or twice a month at least, in the year to the markets and the fairs. Here any man who paid his dues on what he sold or bought had a right to be present, as long as he kept the peace.

It is true that sometimes when the king was weak, and his servants were negligent or corrupt, crime was frequent and there was danger. But the danger was mainly to strangers and travellers, and the people felt but little interest, except occasionally, in these risks.

Another reason why the acts of government were criticized and, if need be, resisted, was the fact that all taxation was what people now call direct. The dues payable to king and lord were contributions from the actual substance of those who were taxed. The property which each man had was, so to speak, ransomed, for if he would or could not pay, his goods could be seized and sold, so that his dues should be paid. To be sure, the dues were fixed, and were payable at given dates, always carefully recorded, so that he was warned of his liabilities beforehand.

Hence every man resented strongly any attempt on the part of the Exchequer to enlarge or extend the liabilities to the central authority. It is possible that individuals were oppressed, especially if they were unpopular. It is certain that no Englishman cared much if the foreigner was plundered; and if the Jew was mulcted, he not only did not care, but was rejoiced. It was a very different thing, however, if any attempt was made to revise and increase the fixed charges which the tenant had to pay. One attempt of this kind (1381) shook the government to its foundations, and nearly led to a revolution. It was never tried again.

Again, as all Englishmen, from the highest to the lowest, were either directly or indirectly amenable to this Exchequer, it was obvious that all classes made common cause against it if it overstepped its rights. The noble did not resist the just claims of the crown. It would be unwise to do so, as the example might be catching. But every one was interested against what might be the common enemy.

When John was forced to sign the great Charter at Runnymede (1215), the whole nation, from the earls to the peasants, was against him. He had hired a foreign army, and he thought he could trust the authority of the Pope, who, as he well knew, would protect him. But his foreign soldiers were cowed, and the man whom the Pope had forced on him, Stephen Langton, the Archbishop of Canterbury, was as zealous for the English as the nobles were, as the land-owners and yeomen were, as the burghers of London and other towns were. And when he signed the Charter, and afterwards, relying on

the Pope's authority, strove to recall or rescind
it, he found that the English still resisted, and
the Pope found that he could not maintain his
pretensions, as all the nation was against him.
He was therefore wise enough to yield to the
circumstances which he could not control.

These times are called dark ages. There is
no doubt that many of the things with which we
are familiar were unknown then. But that of
which people have had no experience cannot be
a loss to them. In all essentials of spirit and
character, the England of five or six centuries
ago was the England of to-day. It is easy to
show how great were the deficiencies of the life
which our forefathers lived, and how violent a
contrast it was with that in which their descendants now live.

But it is even more certain that the English
people would never have been what it now is,
if it had not, even in these early days of its
history, possessed in itself all the powers and
many of the processes which characterize the
modern history of our experience. It demanded
good government and fair dealing from its rulers,
and it took the very roughest and most effectual
means, according to its opportunities, to secure
what it wanted.

Foreigners were so surprised at the English
spirit and the energetic resistance of the people
to bad rulers and wicked ministers, and at the
people going to extreme lengths when their
wrath was fairly roused, that we got the name

of the *disloyal nation*. Nothing could be more unjust. What the English people wanted was loyalty all round, loyalty of the king to the law and his people, loyalty of the people to honest, just, and wise government. And as long as this sense of mutual duty was affirmed and acted on, matters were sure to come right in the long run.

CHAPTER IX.

THE KING'S COURTS.

I HAVE spoken of the Exchequer as the watchful guardian of the king's rights. Its machinery was, as I have said, that of the village court on the most extended scale. It strove in the highest department of state to treat the nation collectively as every parish or settlement or manor was treated within its own boundaries. It had many temptations to do wrong. The machinery by which it could be controlled was rough and imperfect, and ages had to elapse before the machinery could be made smooth, regular, and effective. But I repeat it never was an arbitrary despotism.

Now let us see what good it did, apart from its mere machinery of action, which, as I said, was continually instructing the nation in the necessity of common purposes, in carefully watching after that which might do wrong.

I have already adverted to one of those

services—a service which sprang from the incidents of the Conquest. It took the duty of inquiring into homicide where the culprit was unknown, out of the hands of the local authorities, and performed that duty itself. Where this offence, like other offences, was committed in parish or manor, and there was no doubt about the offender, at first, and for a long time, the punishment was left to the locality.

The maintenance of the king's peace was exercised over places which were out of the local jurisdiction; over the king's highway, in the wastes, and in the forests. People are surprised at the severity of the forest laws. But this severity did not affect the mass of the people. Honest people lived in the villages. Those who habitually resorted to the forests and lived there were highwaymen and thieves, and, according to the theory of justice at the time, should be dealt with quickly and sharply. You may depend on it that there was little moan over those whom the king's rangers caught and put out of the way, or, according to the hard usage of the age, when there were few prisons, maimed and therefore disabled from unlawful practices. In those times, a poacher in the king's forest was a robber, who, when he could not pillage wayfarers, got his living by stealing deer. The ordinary English peasant had abundance of game, which he snared, or trapped, or netted, or hawked, and either put into his pot or sold to the squire or abbot. As late as the seventeenth century, country nobles and gentlemen purchased weekly during the winter, enormous quantities of what we should now call game. These must have been captured by the small farmers and the peasantry.

It is true that a forfeiture of goods, if a man were convicted of a capital felony, accrued to the king, or to the lord, in case the latter had such a franchise or right, and that the coroner, who took the earliest steps on behalf of the crown when homicide was committed, was bound to return evidence as to the goods of the culprit. But the goods of such people as committed these offences were rarely worth much, and there was no such eagerness to procure these convictions as there was to obtain convictions for treason, the offenders in the latter case being generally persons of high rank. But it must be remembered that the king paid the judge's salary out of his own personal revenue, and, as I have said before, the essence of the relations between superior and inferior in these times was that the king did a service, and the person benefited by the service paid for it. This is substantially the case now. A government is supposed to fulfil the most important functions in protecting life and property, and in keeping the peace. On these grounds it collects taxes from the people.

The officers of the king's Exchequer were also engaged in doing justice between man and man, especially in litigation when the rights of property were the stake. As I have stated

above, the record of ownership within the parish
or manor was provided for by the jury of freeholders, and the register of the tenants, by the
symbolical acknowledgment of possession, and
by the notorious character of the act, under
which that acknowledgment was effected. But
there were other and much more important
matters, as far as the magnitude of the interests
was concerned, to be dealt with. There were
lawsuits between parties as to the property
which a great landowner might have in the
manor, which no local jury, and not even a
county court, could decide. In such cases, the
king's court was entreated to settle the question.
It undertook this business, on the payment of
certain fees, and its decision was final. In
course of time, when persons wished to sell an
estate they found that the notoriety which the
court gave, and the authority of its decision,
was the best security which property could have,
and so they set up in this court what were called
fictitious actions, *i.e.* pretended suits of law
which were well understood only to mean, that
the Court, as it was called, of Common Pleas,
witnessed the transaction. In this manner, by
taking heed to the king's revenue, by keeping
the king's peace, by doing justice between man
and man, and by registering the titles to estates,
the Exchequer made itself felt, and not without
public advantage, in a vast number of familiar
and general transactions.

Here, then, was an institution of government.

ever watchful, ever present, bent on securing the personal interest of the king, and yet able to confer great benefits on the public, of which the greatest, though it was not recognized, was the right of criticizing the conduct of the government sharply. If a mere private individual ventured on such a course—and there was no great opportunity for him to do so in early times, and for the matter of that, till very recent times—he might be very harshly treated, unless his opinion had a great following. Even in the most despotic periods of English history, the king has not ventured to take his people's goods without their consent, or violate common and cherished rights. Unpopular persons and crude opinion he could chastise, or even oppress.

It is a common saying that the best government is that which, whatever be its forms, gives the largest possible amount of liberty, and secures the most exact and perfect order. The problem is, how can this harmony be secured. One may see that a result is good, one may wish that the result should be arrived at, but this is very different from obtaining the result, from discovering how far the power should go, and how the check to an abuse of the power should be applied. Order without responsibility may, and a hundred times does, degenerate into frightful oppression—oppression which cankers the very life of the people. Liberty at its best, if it has a weak common object, and a strong personal object, may split up society into fragments, and be fatal to national life and patriotism, because it weakens the sense of public duty. If the central government becomes overwhelmingly strong, if it undertakes to direct not only the conduct of affairs, but the life of the individual, the more honest and sure it is, the more does it kill individual enterprise. If it be harsh and selfish, it will become a great evil, and it may destroy the nation itself.

Now in England, and from the earliest times, there was a powerful government. Occasionally the ruler was weak and incapable, and disorders of no common magnitude ensued. Except, however, in one reign, that of Stephen (1135–1154), there was no anarchy.

But this government was always open to criticism, rough at times, and violent, but effective. If the king had his rights, they were definite, and the subject had his rights too. There was a bargain between the parties, not avowed or defined in words, but just as real as though the contract were reduced to writing, and signed by the parties. Three times in English history, it was reduced to writing. These were, in the Great Charter (1215), in the Petition of Right (1628), and in the Bill of Rights (1689). It was very unsafe to traverse this mutual understanding, and to break faith.

CHAPTER X.

THE ENGLISH TOWNS.

THE population of the English towns was about one-eighth that of the country districts. But at a very early date these towns got the privilege of self-government, *i.e.* of municipal institutions, under which they elected their own magistrates, assessed their own taxes, in order to pay the king's rent and to meet their local needs, and dealt with their own interests.

Of these towns by far the most opulent and powerful, even in early days, was London. It was strong by nature and by art. It was on a high bank rising from the Thames, protected on the west and east by streams, then easily defensible, and on the north by extensive marshes. At the Conquest, it made terms with William. It is said that the Tower was built in order to overawe it. It certainly never was overawed.

There is no date assignable to the liberties and self-government of London. Plenty of dates may be given for the enlargement of its privileges and self-rule. It is probable that it was a municipality from Roman days, and that it had never lost the form which it had. It was an open market with large privileges from time immemorial.

There were frequent uprisings against the government, for, as I have hinted, in rude times insurrection took the place which plainly expressed popular opinion takes now. Whichever side London took was victorious in the end, and sometimes quickly. The Conqueror, as I have said, treated it with marked favour. It put Stephen on the throne. It had a great hand in forcing John to sign the Great Charter. It took the lead in resisting the mismanagement of his son. It deposed Edward II. (1327), Richard II. (1399), and Henry VI. (1461). It raised Richard III. (1483) to the throne. It took the side of the Parliament against Charles, and it really was the strength which deposed his son James. The city of London put the house of Hanover on the throne, and kept it there.

And yet the municipal institutions of this wonderful city, whose history, if it were properly written, is more remarkable than that of any other city in the world, not excepting Athens and Rome, were not essentially different from the picture of self-government which every village in England exhibited. The people managed their own affairs in the villages, and though they did not often elect their own head man, the parson, *i.e.* the person of the village, or the rector, *i.e.* the ruler, or administrator, the chairman of their local parliament, the vestry, or assemblage of rate-payers, still the goodwill of the parishioners was very essential or advantageous to the comfort of the head man.

F

The municipal institutions of London were copied in other cities and towns. Shortly after the Conquest, the bishops transferred their seats or sees from poor villages to opulent or growing towns. Only one of these persons kept to the little village in which his see was originally planted, and Ely, the place in question, still remains a hamlet.

These prelates materially aided the growth of the towns to which they migrated. Sometimes, as at Salisbury, they created the town. Sometimes they occupied the old town, and made the inhabitants take up with an area near them, as at Lincoln. Sometimes they created a second walled town in which they and their establishment lived, as at Norwich. It is common fairness to say that they did their best to further the material interest of the town in which they dwelt.

Very rapidly, then, for the creation of these municipalities was the work of a century, there grew up over England communities with representative institutions, and with acknowledged and well-defined rights. These rights, in the sight of violent men, who had been accustomed to licence, and had seen abroad what war might do to ruin nations, were humble or even contemptible; but the king found very soon, and his advisers, especially his legal advisers, saw that there was no power more valuable for curbing lawlessness than these towns were. They were all on the side of order, and enemies

of violence, except that which they committed
themselves, in order, as they sometimes justly
thought, to secure their imperilled liberties.
So there grew up a doctrine that if a serf could
contrive to live for a year and a day in one of
these walled towns, his master lost all right over
him. It is impossible to think that so extraordinary a breach of feudal law would have been
sanctioned, unless the king and the law had seen
how useful it was to favour these towns, and to
increase their power. If space allowed, I could
show from many facts how anxious the king
was to strengthen those places which had enjoyed such institutions and were centres of
order.

It was not remarkable that the king delegated
authority to the magistrates of the town. The
practice was in accordance with the principles
of the age. The king could not sit in the
court, where every writ ran in his name, and he
was presumed to be present. The lord of a
manor could not sit in his own court, but must
be represented by his steward or deputy. The
difference between the ruler and the magistrate
is engrained in English habit.

The enterprise of the towns, and the power
of access to them, had a great deal to do with
making England a nation. The seaports protected the shores and the merchant shipping of
the country. There are many towns, now decayed and become mere fishing villages, which
at one time were swarming with what were the

best war vessels of the time.   The Kentish and
Sussex towns, called the Cinque Ports (Dover,
Hastings, Hythe, Romney, and Sandwich), saved
England from a foreign invasion more than
once.   They owed their energy to the system
of local self-government.

Very early the mariners of Scarborough ventured to Iceland, off the shores of which were
vast fishing grounds.   Long after this the
Bristol shippers trusted to the mariner's com-
pass, and as the Scarborough men reached
Iceland through the comparatively quiet seas of
the German ocean, these men were bold enough
to dare the Atlantic on the same errand, and
reached their end.

The making of a citizen is in his courage.
His own interest, maybe, guides him first.
But as a general on a campaign assures himself
as far as he can of a friendly country, but, above
all, resolves to secure the base of his operations,
so these venturesome men took care that crown
and law should be respected, and that they
should have the goodwill of their own neighbours.   There can be no sustained courage in
the midst of permanent enemies.   A man may
be resolute, and despairingly so, but he cannot
have the courage of progress.

The attachment which these townsfolk felt
towards the place of their birth, their bringing
up, and their fortunes, was keener than we can
have, perhaps, any notion of.   The Londoner,
from the cradle to the grave, inhabited the same

house, frequented the same exchange and guild-house. London was not then, as it is in our days, entirely built over. The streets were narrow, and the houses mean, but they had large gardens in their rear. There were many open spaces in the city—the grounds of the numerous monasteries, and the markets. Above all things the citizen of the time valued his own urban institutions, his liberties, and his electoral rights. The same was the case with the other great towns of England—York, the capital of the north, Norwich of the east, where the principal manufactures of old England were carried on, and Bristol, the chief city of the west. But there were numerous other towns with their charters of self-government, and their local interests. They were centres of political education, of commercial activity, and of progressive energy.

CHAPTER XI.

THE SERFS AND THEIR ENFRANCHISEMENT.

THE mass of the English people was divided after the Conquest into two classes, the free and the serf. The distinction between these two orders consisted in the fact, that in theory the latter could not rise to the condition of the former, but must remain disabled unless his lord formally gave him his liberty. In course of time, however, the distinction between the two orders disappears, and serfdom insensibly vanishes.   Let us try to make out the process by which this change was brought about.

It is quite possible that originally the serf was absolutely a slave, a person who had no rights against his lord, had no property except at his lord's will, and could be constrained to labour for his bare maintenance.   But from the beginning, though he was a slave to one man, he was free towards every one else, *i.e.* had rights as against everybody but one person. No serfdom in England was ever like negro slavery, the slavery of a race.   The serf was of the same blood and stock with the free man and the lord his master, of the same faith, worshipped in the same church, and was buried in the same graveyard.

The first step in his emancipation was the powerful force of custom.   Custom and the limitation of rights over others were the fundamental part of English life.   Everybody was liable in some way to his neighbour—the noble by military service, the freeholder by a fixed rent, the monk and the priest by their prayers and religious offices, but always only to a fixed and definite amount.   I have seen many instances in which a religious body has received a grant of land, on condition that certain services should be regularly performed, and in which the frequency of these services was as exactly defined in proportion to the value of the gift as in our own day a farmer might bargain as to the amount of the rent which he should pay for his holding. It was impossible that a large section of the community should be debarred from the advantages of custom. Every one else held on conditions, and at last conditions were granted to the serf. These conditions fulfilled, he was left to employ the rest of his time as he would, and to dispose of his extra earnings as he pleased.

His labour was fixed, his money payments, or payments in kind, were fixed in the earliest records of manors which I have seen, and I believe exist. If he does not labour, he pays a money due instead; and if one were to reckon up his payments in labour, in money, and in kind, it would be found that he held his land on much the same terms as the freeholder did.

His further emancipation was materially assisted by two very powerful forces, the Church and the Law, if indeed much distinction could be made between the two, for the lawyers of the time almost invariably were taken from the clergy. Both of them interpreted law and custom, or enforced justice to the serf, on any occasion which was convenient.

The Church welcomed the serf and admitted him to her vast privileges and authority. So freely was he allowed to enter into orders, that Henry II., who strove to raise or extend the authority of the crown against the privileges of the Church, insisted in those famous constitu-

tions of Clarendon, which were the first cause of
his quarrel with Becket, that serfs should not be
ordained without the lord's consent. The greatest
divine, scholar, and Churchman (Grostête) of
thirteenth-century England sprang from this
despised order.

Poverty was no discredit in this early time.
The great revival of religion which characterized
the period in which these changes were going
on was that of the two orders of begging friars
(1210), the Franciscans and Dominicans. These
missionaries revived the almost forgotten practice
of preaching. By their vows they could have
no possessions. The older orders had lands,
houses, money ; and the heads of the great
abbeys vied with bishops and nobles in wealth
and pomp. But the two new orders did not
even possess the hovels in which they were
lodged. Hence they were held in great honour,
and were treated with confidence. These
zealous preachers, wherever they went, advo-
cated the natural equality of man, by dwelling
on the infinite inferiority of all men in the sight
of God, and urged that nothing could be more
acceptable than justice to others.

The clergy, we are told, advised their penitents
to manumit their serfs, though our informant
adds somewhat spitefully, that they did not act
in their own possessions on the advice which
they gave so freely to others, and that even at
the time of the Reformation a nominal serfdom
existed on many of the abbey lands. But it

became a common practice for the lords to give licences of non-residence, and to manumit for very small sums of money. The last payments which I have seen made for the marriage of daughters and for non-residence on the manor are in the fifteenth and early part of the sixteenth centuries. The working classes were very prosperous during the fifteenth century, and when they were still under these obligations they appear to have bought up their dues.

The action of the king, too, must have had its effect. From early times, the king provided himself on occasion with a personal army, enlisted and specially drilled, and distinct from the national militia of freeholders. It was with this army that the wonderful victories were won in France against such prodigious odds at Crécy, Poitiers, Agincourt, and elsewhere. It was on the model of this ancient army that Cromwell picked and drilled his Ironsides, and, again, that Marlborough and Wellington formed the troops with which they fought, to say nothing of similar feats of discipline and endurance which have characterized British armies in other parts of the world.

Though the serf was not enrolled in the militia, he could and did enter into the royal army. We learn by accident that one of the most valiant of Edward III.'s captains, who had been knighted by him, and put into an office of great trust, was born a serf, and had fought his way up to fortune and rank. Now the age of

Edward III. was one in which the pride of birth was arrogant to an extreme, and it may be doubted whether there was any other country in Europe but England, in which a serf could have risen to the dignity of a kinght, for knighthood put its recipient almost on a level with the king's peers—if, indeed, a noble who had not received knighthood was not inferior to a commoner who had.

In this manner the condition of the lowest class in society was gradually rising. In other countries it was more and more depressed. The French peasant was made to bear all the weight of taxation, till he became, perhaps, more miserable than any one in the world. Nor was the condition of the German peasant better. After the great change which came over the course of European trade, when Egypt in 1516 was conquered by the Turks, and the Cape passage became the only road which remained open for the commerce of the East, the sources of that wealth which was so considerable for Italy and the Flemish towns were dried up, and the nobles began to oppress the German peasant. The peasants rose in rebellion, were vanquished, and were thrust down into more hopeless servitude.

A century and a half before this time (1358), the French peasantry tried to better their condition by an insurrection, in which they were also defeated and driven into a lower position than they even occupied before. In both cases, though there was war going on, the combatants suspended their hostilities and combined to put down the outbreak. These were the only occasions in which the common people, as they were called in these two countries, tried to better themselves by force of arms, until, of course, the terrible uprising of the French Revolution (1789).

In England, however, there occurred an insurrection (1381) from which, though it collapsed and was to all appearances a failure, results of the most important kind ensued, results which entirely modified the domestic history of this country, and led to the virtual emancipation of the serfs.

The only relic of the ancient system which has survived to our day is the tenure which is known as copyhold. In this tenure, the manor court registers successions and conveyances. It is not at all unlikely that such an evidence of title was an advantage, for even now, though a copyholder may compel the enfranchisement of his estate, many estates of this kind still exist. In ancient times the occupancy of such property marked the social condition of the holder, but as early as the fifteenth century it only indicated certain pecuniary liabilities.

CHAPTER XII.

THE EVENTS WHICH ASSISTED THE SERF.

I SHALL now attempt to point out by what course of events the English serf became virtually free, apart from those influences and tendencies which have been stated above. The circumstances may be exactly traced, and though complicated, can all be discovered and be assigned their several forces.

It will be remembered that labour rents were generally convertible into money payments at an early period. In course of time they were universally so commuted, these payments being a little less than the ordinary rate of wages payable for the service. These payments became part of the regular income of the superior lord, and are always entered as the first item of his income in the annual balance-sheet which was always made up on every estate ; these balance-sheets still exist by thousands in public and private collections.

When everything of this kind had long been settled and acknowledged, Europe was visited (1348) with a prodigious calamity in the form of a destructive pestilence. It treated every country alike, and it is calculated, with great probability, that a third of the people perished within a few months. The consequence was a

very great rise in the price of labour and for
everything which had to be bought, with the
exception of food, which, of course, as there were
fewer mouths to consume it, did not feel the
same rise. In consequence, the profits of the
more opulent landowners and agriculturists fell
to next to nothing. They were forced to
abandon agriculture, and to let their land and
stock together on the best terms they could.

They tried to regulate the wages of their
hands by act of Parliament. But the law,
though re-enacted again and again, was not
powerful enough to arrest the rise. They could
not get back to the old rates of wages even for
the farm hands, and were of course powerless
to control the price of whatever else they needed
to buy for the cultivation of their fields. Besides,
the labourers combined together, and when the
law fined some persons—few we may conclude
from the whole number who took more wages
than the law allowed—the labourers paid the fine
out of a common fund. Then they fined the
persons who paid more than the customary
wages, a pretty plain proof that the employers,
in whose interest the law was enacted, felt that
they could not attempt to beat down the
labourers' wages with any prospect of success.
Year after year, as we can see from evidence
which exists, and is indisputable, wages went on
rising, and of course the rents of the landowner
went on falling.

At this time, too, a very remarkable religious

movement was going on, and with it, though not perhaps intentionally, a great social movement. I am referring to the effects of Wiklif's teaching and of the instruments which he used.

Wiklif's youth was contemporary with the great plague to which I have referred. He must have been about twenty-five years of age when that appalling visitation took place. It was especially deadly at Oxford, where he was residing. Before this event it was thronged with students. A distinguished person who was flourishing a hundred years after the plague, says that he counted thirty thousand students' names on the register of the University before that event.

Wiklif was as considerable a person in the University as Grostête had been a century before him. His learning, in what was then learning, was abundant, and his reputation was early and great. He had the advantage it seems, too, of considerable social position, for he was a scion of a respectable and well-to-do Yorkshire family.

At this time England was at war with France. Edward III., for reasons which many persons thought valid, claimed the French crown. Whatever the worth of his claim was, it was weakened by the length of time which elapsed between his right (as he interpreted it) accruing and the claim he made.

During this time the Pope was living at Avignon, and had been there for more than forty years. Every pope was a Frenchman, and was supposed to be on the French side of the quarrel. The Pope, therefore, was not so popular in England as he had been when he lived at Rome and was supposed to be impartial on public questions.

People naturally believed that the great Death was a judgment for national sins. Unhappily the calamity was followed by manifest scandals. The clergy, secular and regular, became frightfully demoralized. It has been noticed over and over again that in such calamities men get desperate, immoral, and violent. Even the missionary orders, the friars, fell utterly from their old reputation, and rapidly lost their popularity.

The court of Rome, then at a small town in the south of France, was in great straits. It was poor, and its administration was costly, as it could not employ its servants without wages; and it claimed, and indeed had long exercised, the right of confirming or annulling the nomination to benefices, and had even conferred these benefices in expectancy. It was filling offices in the English Church with men who never came near England, but simply took an income from it. At that time it was said that one-third of the land of England was in the hands of the Church, besides the tithes and dues. The clergy were about one-tenth of the adult inhabitants.

Now, here was plenty of material for discontent. Wiklif was emphatically an Englishman, who thought that the influence of foreigners in England should be shortened to the narrowest limits. He was devout, and was dissatisfied with the morals of the clergy. He was learned in the learning of the time, and he believed that others would be the better for all the learning he could impart to them. So he struck at the Pope's power, at the authority of the monks and friars, and determined to translate the Bible into English, as well as to undertake a literary controversy. His personal popularity, his connections, and the situation of affairs, greatly increased and entirely account for his influence.

He naturally adopted expedients which suited the temper of his time. A century and a half before, the friars were reformers, whose conduct and preaching rebuked the older orders. Now the friars had become no better than the monks. He determined to create a new order of poor priests, who should revive the best age of the friars, who should surpass them in diligence, and should reach the hearts of the people.

Now, at a time when the labourers' wages were rising, and the landowners, in and out of Parliament, were seeking to keep them down by all the means in their power, it was natural that the religious order which Wiklif had created, and named *poor priests*, probably because he wished it to be understood that they were not a monastic order, should be in strong sympathy with the wishes and objects of the working classes. One does not see how they could reach them and influence them, unless they strove to assist them in bettering their temporal condition.

Wiklif does not seem to have laid down any rule for his disciples or agents or emissaries. I make no doubt that he thought it better not to imitate the old orders in this characteristic and invariable feature of their organization. Every order of monks had a rule, or discipline, and was under a regulated authority. So much was this the case that the order itself was often called a rule. Wiklif appears to have thought that no other discipline was necessary than that of religious zeal.

Furthermore, Wiklif himself began to move away more and more from the doctrines of the Roman Church. This is what always happens. They who dispute the authority of any government are always led to examine the grounds on which that authority is founded, and ultimately to challenge the opinions of those who insist that this authority should be respected. Just the same course of events happened a century and a half after Wiklif's time. Henry VIII. and his advisers wished to extinguish the authority of the Pope in England, but to maintain the doctrines of the Roman Church. But events were too strong for them, and gradually there grew up a feeling that the tenets of the Roman Church were as unsatisfactory as its authority.

It does not seem that Wiklif's powerful friends

were greatly offended by the growth of his
opinions. On the contrary, they rather protected him; for it seems that at this time the
wealthy clergy were nearly as unpopular as the
Papal authority was.

CHAPTER XIII.

THE INSURRECTION OF THE SERFS.

I SAID above that the working classes united
together to pay the fines which the law levied
on them for taking higher wages than the law
allowed, and that these unions were, as we
are expressly told by contemporary writers, as
universal as they were powerful. But it was
impossible for the workmen by themselves to
carry out this process or to find the agents for
it. It was the essence of that old society that
every one knew what his neighbour was about.
The whole machinery of local justice was based
on this presumption. Men were held responsible for the misdoing of their fellows to an
extent which we cannot realize, and, in order
to be responsible, it was necessary that they
should know all that could be known of their
neighbours.

But the case was different with the clergy.
They were amenable to Church authority only.
It is true that the king had made good his
authority against them, at least in everything

that was supposed to affect his dignity, or to bring them within the penalties of treason.

Besides, they were expected to roam about, preaching and teaching. There was nothing in the system of Wiklif's priests which was at variance with the practice of the time. On the contrary, they were only doing what the friars had done, with great acceptance, for a long time. The manner of their preaching was very familiar, and as yet they were careful of the matter of their preaching, or perhaps nobody beyond the working men paid much attention to what they said.

It is plain that these poor priests supplied the organization which the work-people could not have created themselves, and were the treasurers of the fund subscribed for common purposes. We come to this conclusion, partly because we know of no other agency which could have been employed, partly because we know that there was a powerful and secret combination, partly because the general judgment of the time fastened on the poor priests the responsibility of the events which followed. They are distinctly said to have preached about the natural equality of man, and to have called in question the claims of superiority which the noble and wealthy classes made, and had for so long a time given effect to.

One of the expedients which the landowners bethought themselves of in this very serious crisis of their fortunes, was a revision of the bargain which they had made with their dependants or serfs long before, when they accepted a fixed sum of money in lieu of labour. In theory, the serf, as the lawyers told them, held at his lord's will. In practice he had, at a period more or less remote, paid for his holding by his labour. His lord had agreed to take money in place of labour. But at the present time the labour cost twice as much as the commutation came to. It was not, they argued, unfair that this bad bargain should be revised, and a new one entered into which was more just to the landlord.

They proceeded to put this plan into execution, and to imprison those who resisted payment. They took the same steps with some of the poor priests who were more imprudently outspoken than others were. The time seemed favourable. The king was a child. His principal guardian, John of Gaunt, had become very unpopular, and his half-brothers, a great deal older than he was, were already distinguished by violence and misconduct.

In an instant, and on the same day, there broke out an insurrection which extended over nearly the whole of England. It is known in history as Wat Tyler's rebellion, but historians have been very much in the dark as to the causes which brought it about, its extent, and its consequences. It was strongest in what was then the wealthiest part of England, the eastern counties. The suppression of it was followed by a long weakness on the part of the government.

The king and his advisers evidently wished, when Parliament met, to get rid of all the conditions of serfage as they existed in their modified form. But the landowners would not hear of this, as was not unreasonable. But no attempt was made again to revive the old money payments. Gradually the estates of the serfs assumed a new form, under the name of copyholds, and these estates, though they often had peculiar customs, were as much secured to the owners as any other.

Custom, therefore, and an insurrection apparently unsuccessful, but really, as far as its purposes went, a complete success, put an end to a system which had long existed, and seemed likely to endure. We do not know how it was that the money rents of the copyholders were extinguished, while other peculiarities connected with their holdings survived. But we do know that within two or three generations of this memorable insurrection, men of family and fortune purchased copyholds, now free from servile taint.

But, on the other hand, in other countries, and especially in France, the lot of the independent cultivator grew worse and worse. A tenant at will, across the channel, was in a far better position than the owner of land under an inferior or agricultural tenure in England, in very early days. In course of time his condition became more miserable and more galling. At last, the most tremendous convulsion that the world has hitherto seen occurred, in which the innocent and the guilty, the just and the unjust, perished in a common ruin. This is called the French Revolution of 1789–1793.

The English people knew who it was who had really wrought this work. The insurrection of 1381 deprived Wiklif of his powerful friends, and he lived on obscurely for three years and a half. His mind was set on political and religious reforms. I mention them in the order in which they occurred to him. His disciples added to them a social reform, carried out, it must be allowed, with culpable violence, but which produced in the end the best results, because at an early date it gave room for the development of the English constitution, by paving the way for the freedom and equality of all Englishmen before the law.

The weight of the reaction and retaliation fell on the poor priests. They were thenceforth persecuted. In order to stop their mouths, twenty years later a law was enacted providing that no clergyman should preach without a bishop's licence, even after he was ordained; and it is alleged that much of the violence and misdoing which brought about the great war of succession between the adherents of York and Lancaster was due to the silencing of the preachers. Wise men, who disliked the reformers heartily, saw that universal repression was an error.

Meanwhile, the artisans of eastern England, where most of the wealth of England was, harboured the preachers of Wiklif's school. One can only get glimpses from time to time of the secret way in which these teachers of the early Reformation kept up their work stealthily and in danger, for the proof of their activity is found only when they were captured and executed. It was specially in Norfolk that these emissaries of the reformed faith laboured, and more sufferers under the heresy laws perished in Norfolk before the time of Henry VIII., and during his daughter Mary's reign, than in all the rest of England besides.

I do not here enter into the merits of the war of succession in the fifteenth century, or into those of the struggle between king and parliament in the seventeenth, but it is remarkable that the geographical line which separated the two contending parties on each of these memorable occasions, was almost exactly the same as that which divided England in the uprising of 1381.

CHAPTER XIV.

THE EARLIEST PARLIAMENTS.

THE English kings were powerful, but never absolute. Probably there never was and never could be an absolute monarch, for a king must act through agents, and then what he calls his

absolute power is really theirs.   I believe that
there cannot be conceived a more painful position than that of a monarch who wishes to do
well by his people, but, being conceived and
admitted to be absolute, is obliged to bear the
unpopularity of those who exercise all his
authority under the shield of his greatness.

Two things always checked the English king,
custom and a council; the former, it is likely,
far more powerful at first than the latter.   His
council was not that of his servants, but of his
critics, perhaps his opponents, occasionally his
enemies, whom he had to consult or to conciliate,
who gave him advice, which might be very un-
palatable, or checked his purposes, which might
be more so.   There were sure to be differences
of opinion in this council, of which the king and
his immediate ministers might take adroit advantage, as happened more than once in English
history, or there might be unanimity which was,
as the case might be, helpful or dangerous.   The
council was originally composed of all the king's
tenants.   In time the smaller tenants were
excused attendance, and only the great ones
summoned.   It was a sign of disaffection, perhaps of revolt, if any of these great persons
refused to attend, or even neglected the summons.

The principal occasion on which the king
needed the attendance of his council was when
he wanted money.   In ordinary times, the king
was supposed to be able to carry on the charges
of government from the revenue of his own

estates, and from the customary dues to which he was entitled. If he wanted extraordinary help—no rare event in unquiet times—he had to ask for it, and to risk a refusal. When the heads of the people compelled John to acknowledge that he could not tax them without their consent, they were only reducing to writing what had been the immemorial custom. But there lurked in this clause what is the origin of all popular power in Parliament, the right of those who were asked to refuse and to give reasons for their refusal.

Even the most headstrong of rulers, as long as he is of sane mind, does not wilfully wish to be unpopular. Hence there are early traces of a system under which delegates were elected in order to assist at the king's council in relation to the king's necessities. At last, after a more than usually severe quarrel with one of our kings, the leader of the reforming party, or at least of the opposition to the king's purposes, bade every county and every considerable town send two or more representatives to that assembly which had gradually got the name of a Parliament. There is little doubt that Simon de Montfort, who summoned this Parliament, intended to get the complicity of the people in his political action and plans, *i.e.* that he summoned the men for debate on politics. There is no doubt that he and his plans were exceedingly popular, for after his death in battle, the people would have worshipped him as a saint,

and his conqueror was obliged to speedily for-
give his followers.

At first there was a taint on the very name
of Parliament. It was connected with the
history of a rebellion and a usurpation, and the
sons of its founder had been guilty of a barbarous, treacherous, and unnatural murder. But
Edward I. was no common king. Thirty years
after—perhaps at an earlier date, but from the
later period the record is continuous—he revived
the elected Parliament. Exactly six hundred
years ago (13 Edward I., 1285) the first Parliament occurs on what is like the modern lines,
and from that time to this an institution has
been continuously, though with interruptions, in
existence, which has been imitated by all civilized
nations.

From the first, these Parliaments were invited
to aid the king and to assent to laws. It is
said that the king's maxim was, that what con-
cerns all should have the consent of all ; and
Edward was bent on making extensive altera-
tions in the common or customary law. At
first he seems to have enacted these changes by
his own authority. Soon, however, he put his
intended reforms before Parliament. At first
the old council and the new representatives sat
together. Very soon, however, though the time
of the change is not known, the two separated.
The old council became the House of Lords or
Peers, and generally sat with the king in what
was called the Painted Chamber. The other

body, which became the House of Commons, sat, when it was in London, in the Chapter House at Westminster. But Parliament often sat in other places besides London, as, for instance, at York and at Oxford, in the latter place as late as the time of Charles II.

We do not know who it was who elected these members. There is no early law defining the qualifications of the electors. Generally the Parliament was summoned in order to make the king a grant in aid of his ordinary revenue, and notice was, therefore, unwelcome. But it is certain that all the owners of property were taxed. The taxing rolls for, say, Edward I.'s time are still in existence, and with a little pains one could make a shrewd guess from them as to the population in those parishes of which the records are preserved. The representatives were paid for their attendance, a custom which continued till the seventeenth century.

The Parliament gradually gained power, especially in weak reigns and in troublesome times. It made the assent of Commons as well as Lords necessary for legislative acts, and was taken into counsel on questions of foreign policy during the first great war with France (1366). In matters which the king did not bring before it, but itself undertook, it presented its own attempts at legislation in the form of petitions, to which the king agreed if he approved of them, or rejected under a civil expression to the effect that he would be advised about it.

The reason why the two houses, the old council and the new commons, were separated early, was manifestly this. The king generally invited these assemblies in order to lay before them his wants and to invite their assistance. Now, the Lords were his council, his peers, and he sat with them, as the sovereign is still supposed to sit on the throne in the House of Lords. There were occasions on which the absence of the king from the chamber where he should sit was interpreted to mean a suspension of business. Now, it was rather invidious to discuss the king's necessities in his presence, and a custom early grew up of referring this matter to the Commons, who made their grants, and returned them to the council of the Lords.

Besides, the constitution of the Upper Chamber was very peculiar and very uncertain. The majority was generally of the clergy, the bishops, and heads of monasteries. The lay peers were summoned very irregularly. In one Parliament there might be ninety or a hundred, in another, even in the next year, not one-fifth the number. But the Commons were always present. They were paid for their attendance, and would have forfeited their wages had they been absent.

It is probable that the Commons selected some one or more of their own number to communicate between them and the king. At last they hit upon the plan of choosing a particular person, who should preside over their deliberations, and should be the channel of all communications between them and the king. He was called the Speaker, because he addressed the king on their behalf.

At last it was fully recognized that no tax could be imposed without the consent of Parliament, and that this consent must be first asked in the House of Commons. Thus the House of Commons is absolute over the whole revenue, and it is from this power of taxation that the Commons have become at last able to undertake practically the whole government of the country.

CHAPTER XV.

THE HOUSE OF COMMONS AND THE ELECTORS.

IT is stated above that we have no early information as to who the electors were. It is probable that, in the towns, the burgesses were allowed to make bye-laws regulating the mode of election, so that, in course of time, there was every conceivable court of electors, from universal suffrage to selection by a very limited number of persons. The towns, too, were of all sizes. Some must have been very poor places from the very first, but as long as the custom of creating new boroughs went on, none of any considerable size were left without representatives. The great towns of later times, such as Leeds, Birmingham, and Manchester, were villages at an earlier period.

Each county sent two knights—Yorkshire no more, and Rutland no less. Two counties were under a peculiar local government, Chester and Durham, and were not represented in Parliament at all. The representatives of the counties were evidently considered superior to those which were sent from the towns. They were paid higher wages, they were occasionally consulted, after and in the absence of their town colleagues, and for a long time the Speaker was always selected from this contingent.

Additions were made to the boroughs, apparently on no intelligible principle. The boroughs in Cornwall, Wilts, and Surrey, were very numerous, and it is difficult to believe that some of these were ever considerable places. The king was supposed to bid them send members at his discretion. Sometimes the town refused to obey the mandate, for the charge of the member's wages was heavy, and was met by taxing the townsfolk. Sometimes the inhabitants petitioned against the costly honour.

The two English Universities, on the other hand, after the Reformation, petitioned Elizabeth for the privilege of representation. The queen rejected their prayer, but James conceded it. This representation was accorded on the ground that under it the king would have the advice of lawyers learned in that branch of jurisprudence which found no favour with the common lawyers, viz. the Roman law.

The nomination of members was made in the counties at the county court, and the election was by a show of hands. It does not seem that a poll was ever demanded or taken, and the sheriff, who was the returning officer, who filled up the writ and returned it with the names into the proper office, must have exercised this discretion, in case there were a plurality of nominations, in deciding who were the candidates favoured by the majority.

We are not told who were the electors, till a statute of 1406 informs us. In that year the Commons petitioned the king that the sheriffs should give fifteen clear days' notice of the election. The petition was granted, and a law, as the custom then was, passed on it. But this was, it seems, only intended to reaffirm and enforce ancient custom, for seven years before a return after six days' notice was acknowledged to be an irregularity, and one that should not be a precedent.

But in this same Parliament, the right to the franchise was decided, after a petition to the effect made by the Commons to the king, to belong to all suitors in the county court and others—a form of words which implies that the act bestowed universal suffrage in the counties. The sheriff and the electors were to seal the writ. The use of seals was universal. The poorest man had his seal, and needed to use it occasionally, for a seal was more important in a document than a signature. One of the commonest kinds of seal among poor persons was a coin. In 1685, when Bunyan feared that he would be again subject to persecution, he made over all his goods by deed of gift to his wife, and sealed the document with a twopenny piece.

It is quite clear that the Act of 1406 conferred a very wide suffrage, and that the privilege was valued and exercised, for in 1430 the Commons petition to the effect that the knights of the shire had been chosen by "outrageous and excessive numbers of people of small substance," and that in future the electors shall have a freehold worth a clear forty shillings annually. It was further demanded that the elected knights should reside in the county which chose them. The petition was granted, and an act passed on it. Ten years afterwards, it is further enacted that the freehold must be in the same county.

This restricted franchise remained the only qualification in the counties till 1832, *i.e.* it lasted exactly four centuries. The change cut away from the parliamentary franchise in the counties, all copyholders, all leaseholders, and all tenants at will. The copyholders were, as I have said, the partially enfranchised serfs. Since the landowners had given up cultivation on their own account, the tenants on leases or at will had become very numerous. There is no reason to believe that the freeholders had increased in numbers.

It may be interesting to discover what kind of qualification that was which remains to this day in the counties. If one takes the ordinary rent of arable land at the time, and this was the best of the cultivable land, we shall find it to have been about sixpence an acre, scarcely ever more, very often less. The qualification is therefore eighty acres of arable land. But it is certain that such a holding involved, on an average, common rights in the common pasture to about an equal extent, for in those days at least half the land in every parish was unenclosed, open, and free for pasture to all the inhabitants. Furthermore, the quantity of the land represented by the value, must be free from all outgoings or charges. This may mean even taxes, it certainly means any rent charge, or due upon the land; and I am pretty sure that when the law was enacted it meant a qualification which was very nearly like what £200 a year for land would be in our day, and that it was quite as infrequent a holding as a freehold estate of £200 a year is now. In course of time the value of land rose considerably, and the qualification sank in value, till at last, in our own days, what was intended to be a powerful barrier against persons of mean fortune, became the means for creating what has been called a faggot vote, or even a fictitious franchise.

During the seventeenth century, Cheshire and Durham, with the cities in them, were admitted to the franchise; and towards the close of that century, the last borough which was newly created was given representatives by Act of Parliament. In 1707, Scotland was incorporated with England. In 1801, Ireland was united to Great Britain, and considerable changes were made in the representation of both kingdoms. But there was no change of any important character in the franchise of the electors, and no steps were taken to transfer representations from decayed towns to new centres of population. The manufacturing industry of England had first been placed in the eastern counties. Thence it slowly extended, and finally migrated to the south and west. At a later period, it moved from its second home to the north-west and north-east of England; and that part of the country which, only two centuries ago, was the wildest and poorest part of the kingdom, is now the richest and most densely peopled.

At last, in 1832, a great change was made, and the towns of the north were enfranchised at the expense of the south. In 1867, a very extensive franchise was given to the inhabitants of the towns. In the past year (1884) the same franchise was given to the inhabitants of the counties, so that now the county folk have obtained the same political rights which they seem to have had during the twenty-four years which elapsed between 1406 and 1430.

CHAPTER XVI.

THE PLACE OF PARLIAMENT IN THE CONSTITUTION.

FROM the very first, the Parliament, particularly the House of Commons, not only met to discuss the king's wants, and the best means by which the wants should be aided, or to debate on business which the king put before them, but to petition the king for such changes in the law as might be deemed expedient, and to receive and debate petitions for the redress of grievances suffered and complained of by private persons. It is an ancient and inalienable right of Englishmen to petition Crown and Parliament for the remedy of wrongs, and, by implication, it is the inherent right of Parliament to discuss these wrongs and suggest a remedy for them.

During the earlier times in which the House of Commons became very powerful, i.e. for the first quarter of the fifteenth century, it generally proceeded to legislate by presenting a petition on some subject. The king granted or refused its prayer: and if the former was the result, the law officers of the crown were entrusted with the duty of drawing up an Act of Parliament in accordance with the terms of the petition. The various statutes were written out on a single roll, and the whole treated as one Act, of which

the particular enactments were called chapters.
A committee of Lords and Commons was often
appointed to be present at the codifying of these
petitions, for complaint was occasionally made
that the king's servants introduced material
changes into the words or the purport of the
petition which had been granted.   To the present day, the work of a parliamentary session
is considered to be one Act, of which the several
laws are so many chapters.

There was a reason why the Commons legis-
lated by petition.   In the first place, they could
in this way get an Act of Parliament without
the consent or action of the Lords.   In this
manner they got the two Franchise Acts of
1406 and 1430.   In the same way the clergy
(1400) procured an Act on their own petition,
under which sheriffs in counties and mayors in
towns were constrained to execute heretics by
burning, though neither Lords nor Commons
had agreed to the petition.   Their prayer, however, became law, and remained a reputed law
till 1676, when it was formally repealed.

In the next place, they were able in this
manner to deal with business which was not
put formally before them by the king and his
ministers.   Parliament had right of speech and
debate.   But it was long doubtful whether this
right extended from matters on which the king
asked their advice or consent to matters in
which he would be offended by their treating
the subject at all.   For a century at least, per-

haps for nearly two centuries, individual members of the House of Commons who ventured on handling subjects which were distasteful to the king and court, were in a condition of peculiar peril. One of the most eminent men in parliamentary history (Sir John Eliot) was imprisoned till death, for words said in Parliament. It was only at the Restoration that the right of speech in Parliament was formally declared to be privileged. Even at present, no motion can be made affecting the rights of the crown without the formal assent of the crown to such an action.

The Houses of Parliament sit for the redress of grievances. Hence any member, due regard being had to decorum and order, may question any minister of the crown on any matter of alleged wrong, and till recently could debate a petition. This latter right was suspended because it was abused, but could be revived if it were required. Since the debates of the House of Commons have been published, the necessity for the discussion of private wrongs in Parliament has been greatly diminished.

In early days, elections were frequent; the House of Commons as elected rarely sitting beyond one session, and that generally a short one. As the principal object of summoning the House was the king's want of money, sovereigns who could contrive to make both ends meet out of their ordinary revenue, had no need to call a Parliament. Thus Henry VII. was wealthy and parsimonious. He was fond of money, but he was not popular, and he did not desire to consult his Parliaments. He reigned for nearly twenty-four years, and he only called seven Parliaments.

But the king could hold a Parliament together as long as he pleased. Henry VIII. kept one together for six years. The Long Parliament of 1640 extorted an Act from the king under which it could not be dissolved without its own assent, which assent it never gave till the Restoration. The Parliament of 1661 sat for sixteen years together before the king dissolved it.

After the Revolution, an Act was passed reluctantly by the king under which Parliaments were to exist for three years and no more. After the accession of the House of Hanover, they were not to last more than seven years. In practice they have lasted on an average, since that time, for about four years.

The government cannot exist without a Parliament. Some of the most important taxes are granted for a year only, and if Parliament did not meet and regrant them, they would cease. The public services of the army and navy are granted for a year only, the discipline of the forces under the name of the Mutiny Act is for a year only, and both would fall to pieces unless Parliament annually renewed them. After money is granted to the service of the crown, it must be appropriated by Act of Parliament, and this Act, though it has become a form, might be made a reality, and the whole of supply might be discussed anew. But no person except a minister of the crown can ask for public money. The responsibility of this action is put on these officials.

The sovereign can dissolve Parliament, *i.e.* the House of Commons. In this manner the government of the day, by whom and through whom the sovereign acts, can keep a check on Parliament. On the other hand, the House of Commons can declare that it has no confidence in the government, and then the government must resign, or dissolve Parliament, and appeal to the country at a new election. Under these circumstances, the crown would be unable to keep in its service any minister or ministers who are distasteful to Parliament and the country, for it would be vanquished assuredly, if it prolonged the struggle.

In this manner, and through his representatives, every Englishman who possesses a vote has an influence and weight in the government of his own country, and not of his country only, but of nations whose numbers far exceed those of our own people, and a certain authority over the numerous colonies which Englishmen have founded or acquired. The key to this influence is in the fact that he supplies the means by which the government is carried on, and assesses through Parliament the costs and charges of public business.

As long as the sovereign was jealous of Parliament and considered it if a necessity yet an evil, whose action it would curtail to the utmost of its power, the House of Commons surrounded itself with privileges, held its debates in secret, and visited with severity those who published its proceedings either in vote or speech. There was a time when all these precautions were necessary. But as soon as perfect freedom of speech in Parliament was accorded, and the political opinions of members were no danger to themselves, the motive for this jealous secrecy was past, and the secrecy itself became a mischief. For a long time, however, the House of Commons clung to its privileges, and relaxed them only after a struggle. But it was seen that the electors had a right to know how those whom they had put into a position of trust discharged their trust, by speech and vote. For nearly a hundred years the speeches in Parliament have been regularly reported. For about fifty years the votes have been published, and the electors have thus been able to form a judgment of the diligence and fidelity with which their representatives have discharged their trust.

CHAPTER XVII.

THE KING'S JUSTICE AND JUDGES.

IT is quite possible for a people to have many and perhaps all the guarantees of public liberty, and yet to have a very imperfect system for the guarantee of private or personal liberty. But to an individual citizen, the right, as long as his actions are innocent, to go how and where he pleases, to buy and sell as he wills, to work and be at rest at his pleasure, and generally to distribute his life as he may choose, is even more important than the security of public liberty, though, to be sure, as soon as public liberties are gone, private liberty is in danger.

The rights of men are of their liberty, their safety, and their property. It signifies nothing whether, as some people say, these are natural rights, or as others, that they are the creation of law. Law should be, and let us hope is, justice and good sense put into writing, and administered by a competent judge, and the law of every civilized community admits that any man who has committed no offence, should be left freedom of action, should pursue his calling and pass his life as securely as possible, and should enjoy his property. The law may call upon him to stake all, if a public emergency arises: to subject his liberty to military authority, to risk his life in

the public defence, and to sacrifice his property
in whole or part for the public service. It is
constantly found that in order to secure the
greater part of one's liberty, one must surrender
some of it. Good manners have been defined
to be a small sacrifice for a great gain.

The first claim which a citizen has is to equal
justice. By acquiescing in the authority of law
and courts of law, we imply that the law will
deal fairly between us and those with whom we
are at variance. Hence they who framed the
Great Charter demanded that justice should not
be sold, delayed, or forbidden. Even the king
should submit to have his claims tried and
decided in a court of law, where he is represented, indeed, but not vested with personal
authority.

The king's judges held these functions. Some
tried suits between subject and subject, some
tried suits between the king's revenue and the
taxpayer, some dealt with crimes or offences
against the king's peace. By means of certain
harmless fictions, all the judges were empowered
to try matters which lay out of their original
sphere, but till latterly certain matters were
always special to the King's Bench, the Exchequer, and the Common Pleas.

At first it appears that the judges were taken
from the clergy. It is not quite true to say
that none but the clergy were educated, but it
is probable that most educated persons were
reputed in some way or other to be clergymen

within the numerous orders of the Roman
Church. There are many well-known instances
of persons, who in times before the Reformation
held dignities in the Church, deaneries, prebends,
or canonries and livings, who were not ordained,
but were married men with secular callings.
Indeed, till the Restoration and before the Act
of Uniformity lay persons were able to hold
benefices. Even now it will be seen, by any
one who examines a clergy list, that the reigning sovereign is a prebendary in St. David's
Cathedral.

However this may be, it is certain that the
early judges conferred great benefits on the
English people. Their rules were very often
technical and narrow, but they were always
favourable to liberty and equity. I am sure
that the process under which the serfs were
gradually emancipated, and their property
secured to them, was mainly due to the English
judges, who did more by their fair action
between man and man, and their honest interpretation of contracts, to inspire respect for the
law, and to teach men a true community of
interests than any other power.

A notable and, for the matter of that, a very
innocent source of royal revenue came from the
administration of civil justice. The judges were
paid by the king out of his private estate. This
was compensated by fees of court. It must be
remembered that pleas could be held in the
manor court, in the hundred court, and in the

county court.   Corporations always had their
courts in which they could hear pleas.   But in
the end, the king's courts absorbed the greater
part of all the business which was originally
transacted in these local courts, not because the
king's judges usurped the business, but because
they did it better.   It is true that sometimes
they compelled the inferior court to submit
to the king's court, but they did so because
the court they coerced could not be trusted,
and because the public voice approved their
action.

It is said, and I can well believe it, that the
English judges in developing their system of
justice between man and man, declined to accept
the civil code of Rome, which Europe generally
adopted, and preferred the customary law of
England, corrected as it was by statute, from
time to time, because the language of the civil
code was slavish and imperial.   The customs
which they upheld were the rules of civil life,
under which a free people lived, and they were
unwilling to refer private rights to the authority
of an arbitrary and despotic power.

These English judges were originally appointed during good behaviour, not during the
king's pleasure.   In other words, as long as
they satisfied the duties of their office they were
not removable.   At a later period, and in an
evil hour for the people first, and for the king
subsequently, they were appointed under the
other phrase, and they became as much the

enemies of the English people as they had been its defence.

The king could not sit in his own court. The judges were his deputies, but they were not to be controlled by him. Once, to his and their serious injury, the king (Richard II., 1387) ventured on claiming a private interpretation of the law from them. They were unwise enough to answer him, and they paid the penalty of the offence with their lives. Their sentence had to be in open court, to which all had access.

The judge had to administer the law of Parliament as well as the common law. Now Parliament may be, and indeed has been, occasionally unjust and unfair, has favoured one class of the community at the expense of others, has been mischievously lenient and been mischievously severe. Human institutions, it is almost a common phrase to say, have human frailties, and when they can enshrine those frailties in a law, they will give and have given the worst force, because the strongest, to illdoing. I am not arraigning unfairly the greatest and noblest institution in England without reason, for if what I say were not true, why has there been need to reform the law? When Sir Samuel Romilly and Sir James Mackintosh began their reforms, there were about two hundred and fifty capital offences on the English statute-books, all originated in the interest of particular kinds of property, i.e. enacted not so much on behalf of the public good, but in order to maintain private rights, or that part of the law which refers to the relations of subject and subject.

I have little doubt that it was because the American people, when they were allowed to be independent, saw the danger that legislative assemblies might have private ends in the enactment of law, that they gave the supreme court of the state, and of the federation, the power, for reasons which seemed good and were avowed, to override and even to disallow acts of the legislature. I have often heard eminent Americans declare that this extraordinary power of the supreme court is the most precious part of their constitution.

Now, in an indirect way, this was what the English judges in early times did. They said that Acts of Parliament were only explanatory of the common law, and could not set it aside. And though such an interpretation was perverted ultimately to mischievous ends, and was made the means of furthering absolute power in evil times, it is still true that there is always a difference between the words of a law and its equitable interpretation.

CHAPTER XVIII.

THE CRIMINAL LAW AND THE JUDGES OF IT.

On the whole, then, the constitution of that court which adjudicated in civil cases between subject and subject was worthy of trust and praise.   Even in the worst times of public justice in England, it was freest from blame. But the same in course of time could not be said for the other two courts.

That court which adjudicated on offences against the king's peace was generally desirous to secure order in the country.   But unluckily, through the rule that the conviction of an offender for felony was followed by a forfeiture of his goods to the crown, unless, indeed, some patron or corporation had a recognized right, it became a matter of interest with the servants of the crown to press for a conviction, and use unfair means for bringing it about.   The accused person was not allowed the benefit of counsel. His witnesses were not examined on oath ; and the counsel for the crown, and sometimes bad judges, did not scruple to comment to juries on what they were pleased to call the unsatisfactory evidence for the defence.

Juries, too, were liable to fine and imprisonment, if they gave a verdict which was distasteful to authority.   In early times, as I have said, the jury were witnesses to the fact, not, as now, judges as to the truthfulness of the witnesses and of the general credibility of the whole case for the prosecution and the defence. Now, as sworn witnesses, they ought to have been made liable for any violation of their oaths, just as any perjured person might be and should be. But to inflict such a penalty on them because they gave a verdict which implied that they were dissatisfied with the evidence alleged against the prisoner was in the highest degree unjust. This risk, however, was put on juries till after the middle of Charles II.'s reign, when a decision of Chief Justice Vaughan relieved the jury from this unfair responsibility.

During the existence of an excessively severe criminal code, which was enacted in the supposed interests of property, the juries materially assisted the efforts of reformers by refusing to convict, very often, it must be admitted, in the face of the evidence, criminals charged with what we should justly call petty offences, but which were visited with the penalty of death on conviction. Now, it must be admitted that such a course of action was mischievous, because it set oath as well as law at nought. But juries were commended for their action, because they showed in this indirect way that over-severe laws defeat their own objects. When juries refused to allow persons to be hanged for shop-lifting, sheep-stealing, and even for forgery, it became necessary to modify the law.

The enormous power which the state prosecution of an offender had in dealing with the
case adversely to the suspected criminal is best
illustrated by an instance. In 1692, a certain
Lord Mohun, with a Captain Hill, attempted to
kidnap a famous actress, Mrs. Bracegirdle. An
equally well-known actor, Mountford, attempted
to protect her, and was murdered by the assail-
ants. Lord Mohun was put on his trial before
the peers, and was acquitted by a majority of
votes. It was a scandalous failure of justice,
and is explained on the ground that Lord
Mohun was a very active Whig, who had been
often employed in military commands, and that
his party was in the ascendant.

Mountford's widow attempted to avail herself
of a right which the law then gave to the
nearest representative of a murdered man, of
prosecuting the offender by means of an appeal,
in which process a peer was tried by a common
jury, and, if convicted, could not be pardoned
by the crown. To save Mohun, the crown
lawyers trumped up a charge of clipping the
coin against her father, one Percival, and got
him convicted. He was sentenced to death.
Mrs. Mountford on this petitioned the queen
for her father's pardon, and, we are told, was
informed that it would be granted if she with-
drew her appeal against Lord Mohun. She
did so, and her father was liberated. There
can be no doubt, looking at the circumstances,
that this was a scandalous abuse of judicial

power, and that law was strained in order to convict an innocent person, and to procure the escape of a guilty one.

The eagerness of judges in criminal cases to obtain convictions, and with them forfeitures to the crown, was certainly due to the rule of law which forfeited the lands and goods of offenders on conviction. But it was further strengthened by an evil habit, introduced by the Stuart kings, of giving the judges patents during the pleasure of the crown, and of ejecting them from their offices if they gave the court dissatisfaction. Some of the best English lawyers were treated in this way, and all but the most upright and courageous were terrorized. Hence at the close of the seventeenth century the worst and the wickedest lawyers were found among the judges, and every one who has written on the subject has commented on their violence and cruelty. It has been well said that Bunyan's description, in the " Pilgrim's Progress," of Faithful's trial at Vanity Fair is not an exaggerated picture of a court of law, when Jeffreys, Williams, or Scroggs presided in it.

At the Revolution the old custom of making out the judge's patent during good behaviour was revived, and a new system was introduced by which a judge is removable only by an address from both Houses of Parliament. Still, their patents became void at the death of the king. This was changed a century and a quarter ago.

The Court of Exchequer watched over the king's revenue, and decided on suits in which the king and a subject went to law about the king's dues. No very loud complaints are made about the administration of justice by these officials till after the Stuart period began, when they became unscrupulous servants of the crown.

In 1608, James had, at the instance of his principal minister, laid of his own authority a new tax on currants. A certain Turkey merchant, Bates, resisted the tax as illegal, and the case was heard in the Exchequer. The judges, for reasons which every one has allowed to be monstrous, gave judgment in favour of the crown, and in consequence a new book of rates was immediately published, which imposed heavy arbitrary duties on every description of merchandise.

From that day the struggle began between king and Parliament which, forty years later, ended in the downfall of the monarchy and the establishment of a republic; for the real question at issue between the first two Stuart kings and Parliament was whether the crown could impose taxes at its pleasure, or must abide by the consent of the nation. The question was, indeed, tried anew in the same court, and with the same result, in the celebrated case of Hampden and the ship-money, when a majority of the judges decided in favour of the crown. It was most unfortunate for the Stuarts that they were so

ill-advised in the instruments of their government.

After the Restoration, the government never
again ventured to assume to itself the right of
arbitrary taxation. Parliament was liberal, trade
flourishing, and wealth grew rapidly. But the
king employed the same unfortunate agency for
increasing his power. He strove to assert that
he could dispense with statutes at his will, when
the law was not concerned with a private right,
and he got the aid of his judges to this interpretation of law, if indeed he was not instigated
to it by them with the promise of a foregone
decision in his favour. He attacked the charters
of the cities and towns, and even reduced
London to submission by the action of his
courts. Had he lived longer, the revolution
which was effected under James would have
begun under Charles. It is true that James
went further than his brother, and was in the
end more friendless than Charles ever would
have been.

During nearly the whole of the seventeenth
century, the English judges, with rare exceptions and on special occasions, were as much the
enemies of the English liberty, and hindrances
to the development of the rights of the citizens,
as their predecessors in the same places for
centuries before had been friends and aids to
them.

CHAPTER XIX.

THE LIBERTY OF THE SUBJECT.

ONE of the most intolerable wrongs which despotism can inflict on men is the power of arbitrary imprisonment without cause shown, and without period assigned for trial and acquittal or punishment. It is and must be competent for a state to detain for a period, or even for a lifetime, persons who are dangerous to others, or who have been convicted of crimes ; and we, in common with other civilized communities, empower judges, on adequate proof, to inflict such sentences.

But the prolonged imprisonment of untried prisoners is a different matter. If the power is permitted to a government, it is certain to abuse it. There are always persons whose opinions are distasteful to existing authority, or whose very presence is disagreeable, if not dangerous ; and if a sovereign or an administration is empowered to confine such persons without open trial, it is perfectly certain that the power will be misused.

It must be remembered, too, that such power is as likely to be abused under what are called republics, as well as under monarchies. There is good reason to believe that the republics of Venice and Genoa, and the free cities of the

Rhine, kidnapped those whom they disliked, and hid them out of sight as frequently as the monarchs of France and Naples did those against whom they took offence.

In France it was easy for any person who was in favour with the court, to procure what was called a *lettre de cachet* from the government, empowering him to shut up in one of the king's fortresses, for an indefinite period, any individual towards whom he entertained a dislike, and against whom he was influential enough to be able to give effect to his dislike. It is said that people even obtained blank orders of this kind, and filled the space in as they willed. Of course the king and his government were even more free to use these expedients.

There is a story that an English ambassador in France, during the year 1752, waited on the minister of state through whose hands this kind of business passed, and found that he was away from the office. As he was waiting his eye fell on a list of persons, written on a paper which lay open on the table, and headed " Prisoners in the Bastile." Inadvertently he looked through it, and on the minister entering the room, he apologized for having accidentally inspected a state paper. The minister assured him that it was of no consequence, and that he made no mystery of the fact.

" Then," said the ambassador, "can you tell me how a person named Gordon, who seems to be a British subject, is found in the list ?" " I have no idea whatever," said the Frenchman, "but I will inquire with pleasure, and the man shall be liberated if he proves to be your countryman." On inquiry he was found to be what the ambassador suspected; but no one knew why he had been put in prison, and the prisoner least of all. He only knew that thirty years before he had been suddenly arrested, why, he did not know, and never could guess, and had been a prisoner all this time. The knowledge that the French government had used this system of arbitrary arrest was universal at the time of the Revolution. It led to the destruction of the Bastile, and contributed not a little to that blind and ferocious terror which led to so many enormities afterwards.

In the same way, nearly a generation ago, Mr. Gladstone discovered that a similar system was being practised by the King of Naples on some of his political opponents, men of blameless character and great parts. The conduct of the Neapolitan government was exposed, and the cruelties inflicted on the state prisoners fully described. There is no doubt that the detestation which these acts aroused led to that uprising, the sequel of which was the dethronement of the Italian Bourbons, and the annexation of South Italy and Sicily to the kingdom of Italy.

Now, from very early times, imprisonment without trial was held by the most ancient writers on English law to be illegal. There

was a writ which was intended to obviate the
malpractice. In the Great Charter there is
an enactment that no freeman should be imprisoned without the lawful judgment of his
peers, or by the law of the land. The circuits
of the judges on criminal business were known
as a gaol delivery, *i.e.* the purport of their
appearance at the assizes was to take cognizance
of all imprisoned persons, to try them for the
offence alleged against them, to punish them
according to law if they were found guilty, and
to set them free if they were acquitted. To
keep a prisoner with a charge hanging over him
for an unlimited time was contrary to the genius
of English law ; still more to keep him in
custody with no such charge.

When Edward II. and Richard II. were
deposed, they were imprisoned by order of Parliament, both in view at once of the offences
which they were reputed to have committed,
and for considerations of public safety. It is
possible that both these deposed kings were
murdered by the hands of those who deposed
them. This, if it happened, was the crime of
the administration, but not the intention of
Parliament.

Later on, however, and as a consequence of
the bitter hatred and feuds which had been
created and fostered during the war of succession, the practice of imprisoning those who had
offended the sovereign, or were an object of
alarm to the sovereign, became more general.

Thus Henry VI. was imprisoned in the Tower after his capture in the North, though his only offence was that he had been a rival of the new king. The Earl of Warwick, Clarence's son, was imprisoned in the Tower from his childhood, and was finally executed on a charge of trying to escape. Courtenay, one of the descendants of the Yorkist family, was similarly kept in custody, till he was released by Mary Tudor. Elizabeth imprisoned Hertford and his wife, Lady Katharine Grey, for no other crime than that of marrying against her will; and James treated his kinswoman, Arabella Stuart, with the same illegal severity. The victims of the High Commission Court and the Star Chamber, though these were legally constituted bodies, were conceived to be also unlawfully used, when they were imprisoned. Nor did the Puritans behave more generously. Laud was imprisoned several years before he was brought to trial, and was certainly punished by a court which had no legal authority. Unfortunately, in the early part of Charles I.'s reign, the judges in the Court of King's Bench, who, as I have said, were very much deteriorated from their former high reputation, decided that they could not grant the proper writ, even though a prisoner were committed without any cause assigned, in case he were committed by the special command of the king, or of the lords of the Privy Council.

Though legislation negatived this judgment, the judges continued to evade their duty, till at last, in 1680, the famous Habeas Corpus Act was passed. This, as is often said, created no new law. What it did was to make it perilous or impossible to disobey the law. It inflicted a penalty of £200 for the first offence, and £200 and permanent disability for the second, on any gaoler who offended against its provisions. It put a penalty of £500 on any judge who refused to issue the writ. It put a similar penalty on any person who carried a prisoner out of the kingdom, and in various ways secured to persons a speedy trial.

This Act, reckoned to be one of the most important in the statute-book, was carried by the exertions of the last man who would have been thought likely to have busied himself with it, the first Earl of Shaftesbury, one of the worst men of a very bad age, the reign of Charles II. It is perhaps not unfair to say that, as he had made himself out of favour with the king, he had some eye to himself in what he undertook.

CHAPTER XX.

EDUCATION IN EARLY TIMES.

THERE is a very general idea that people were very uneducated during the whole time which preceded the Reformation, or that at least the clergy only had any culture and intellectual training. It must be admitted that the greater part of what we should now call the educated classes were, in early times, and generally down to the Reformation, ranked as clergy, and had taken what were called minor orders in the Church. The lawyers, the doctors, the architects, the scribes, and the accountants of the time were almost always described as clergymen. But they were very often married men, and this without reproach or scandal.

But it cannot be true that education was confined to these persons. There was not a single manor in England, put under the charge of a bailiff, for which there was not yielded and transcribed yearly an accurate and minute balance-sheet, in which all expenditure and all receipts were carefully noted down, stock taken to the smallest particulars, and the whole audited and checked. No man's head could have carried all these items, and no system of tallies would have sufficed for such scrupulous and punctilious care.

There were several institutions from which knowledge in what then constituted learning could be derived. These were the parochial clergy, the monasteries, and, above all, the universities. In an estimate of the population given towards the close of Edward III.'s reign (1377) the clergy are set down as ten per cent. of the population.

As a rule, every English parish contained an endowed minister who was, by the discipline of the Roman Church, debarred from domestic ties,

was educated for his function, and was possessed
of considerable leisure, even after the work of
his parish and the superintendence of his glebe
lands were completed. It was the peculiar
function of such persons (and they became and
remained, even in the worst days of the old
Church, the best of the clergy) to be the peace-
makers of the parish, the referees in disputes,
and the teachers of the young. We have con-
temporaneous evidence as to the good offices
which they had effected for generations, and of
the services which some of them still rendered.
These persons not only selected for special
training bright and intelligent boys for the
higher learning, but, in order to do so, must
have given some general learning to the whole
youth of the parish. Sometimes an opulent
parish clergyman constantly found the means
for sending selected youths to the universities
for higher and fuller training.

I have often found, in searching among the
relics of pre-Reformation papers, bills for work
done, written out by country artisans, smiths,
carpenters, masons, and the like, in which the
spelling is better than it was three centuries
later, and the charges are properly calculated.
Such persons must have had some education in
reading, writing, and arithmetic.

The age in which Wiklif began his reforms
was by no means a hopeful one. The country
had been terribly demoralized by the great
plague. But he set himself to translate the

Bible into English, certainly not for the prelates
and the clergy, but for the common people. Now,
the artisans of the eastern counties could hardly
afford to purchase the whole Bible, but we are
told that they transcribed and cherished fragments of this version, hid them carefully, and
kept them as dear as life. They must have
known how to read them. We can hardly conceive any relish for a scroll of paper or parch-
ment which was unintelligible to them.

Again, two generations after Wiklif's death,
an English bishop (Pecok) incurred great unpopularity and finally condemnation, because he
wrote, though against Wiklif's followers, con-
troversial books in English. These books, set
out at the very time when printing was being
invented in Germany, were intended for lay
readers, and we may be sure, from the tone they
took, for readers who belonged to the class in
which Wiklif's writings were studied and prized.
They were certainly not intended for the clergy,
since these authorities were grievously offended
at the publications, though the books were intended to justify them and their order and their
doings.

The English monasteries, especially those of
the Benedictine orders, were specially charged
with literary duties. There is no doubt that
they held schools to which the town youth
resorted. Antiquaries still point out the places
in the cloister where the monks of Westminster
held their school, and what they did was done

by other and similar monasteries in the kingdom. Those centres of culture were numerous in the towns, and not infrequent in country places, so that it would not be difficult for an ambitious youth to get beyond the education which the parish priest supplied him with.

The girls, too, were taught in the nunneries, not perhaps quite so numerously as the boys were, but still to some extent. I have seen accounts of these institutions, from which I have found that regular sums were paid for board, lodging, and teaching in those places. When the great revival of learning was brought about in England at the beginning of the sixteenth century, women studied the new learning as eagerly as men did ; and it is probable that Jane Grey and Elizabeth, whose acquaintance with languages, living and dead, was equal to that of men, were only types of a proficiency arrived at by many of their sex.

There were poets, too, who wrote in English for Englishmen. Sometimes, like Chaucer, they contemplated a very large audience ; sometimes, like the author of " Piers Plowman," they wished to undertake the more dangerous task of calling attention to the vices and shortcomings of privileged orders. They would not have written except for readers, and in the latter case for readers among the lower middle classes.

While reading an enormous number of papers written in the Middle Ages and after the Reformation, nothing has struck me more forcibly

than the decline in general education which
marks the later period. A bold, plain, legible
hand degenerates into an almost illegible scrawl,
into very bad grammar and worse spelling. The
common handwriting of Elizabeth's reign is
much harder to make out than that of Henry's,
and in that of the early Stuarts it is even worse.

The destruction of the monasteries, I am
convinced, was a very serious shock to learning.
Much worse, however, was the impoverishment
of the clergy, and the new system of ecclesiastical government and order. The administration, it is true, pretended to check the
mischief, and promised to employ the wealth of
the monasteries for the advancement of learning. But the king broke his word ; perhaps he
was too much pressed for money to keep it.
Some few foundations were made, more were
projected, but all languished.

One of the expedients which was adopted
was to put an obligation on the grantees of
abbey lands, to endow schools out of a portion
of that which they received. Hence, in the
early days of Edward VI., the principal bills
passed in Parliament were private Acts for the
endowment of schools founded by the allottees
of abbey lands. The old centres of local education had been destroyed, and something was
needed to take their room. At first the endowment was small, inadequate, and had but little
effect. In course of time, however, in many
places, land originally of trifling value has multi-

plied a thousandfold, and the present generation, though not always the proper person, enjoys the proceeds of a revenue which the original founder neither contemplated nor intended.

CHAPTER XXI.

THE ENGLISH UNIVERSITIES.

THE origin of the English universities is very obscure. It has been rendered more obscure by an absurd quarrel between the Oxford and Cambridge antiquaries as to the priority of the foundation of either. Even if the question could be settled, it would be unimportant. It is sufficient to know that they are closely connected with that extraordinary revival of intellectual activity which spread from Italy to western Europe during the eleventh and twelfth centuries. We know that there were students gathered in Oxford before the last quarter of the latter century, and that there was an active institution there before fifty years had elapsed from the first notice of Oxford University.

From the first, the universities found favour with the Pope. From the first the universities found favour with the king. But the king wished to bring all the clergy under the authority of the law, while the Pope wished to maintain that the clergy should be free from every lay tribunal. Both granted the universities independence, the king from the authority of his own courts, the Pope from the jurisdiction of his own bishops.

In the struggle between Church and king, which began in the eleventh century, the two powers were naturally anxious to find allies in the new activity which was becoming visible and powerful. The Pope would hope to find the defence of his pretensions in a body which was recruited from the clergy, and which would train the clergy ; the king expected to obtain support from Englishmen on whom he had conferred ample privileges, and who might be expected to prefer independence to deference towards a foreign authority, even though that person might be the pontiff who claimed such rights over princes.

In the estimate of the various forces which have contributed to the slow development of English liberty, we shall constantly have to recognize the aid which was given by powers whose very existence seemed inimical to liberty, and whose policy appears to be inconsistent with it. The Roman Popes, from the early part of the eleventh to the latter part of the thirteenth centuries, were genuine rulers of mankind, who aided most materially in the growth of civilization. They were austere, resolute, active men, who were bent on waging war against anarchy and violence. Their weapons were the extraordinary influence they possessed by reason of the reverence in which their office was held,

K

its splendour, its antiquity, and its pretensions, and the aid of the new intellectual movement. They could dispense with neither of these forces. If the latter had been arrayed against them, it would have soon disputed the former, as it did in the fourteenth century in England, and in the sixteenth in Germany. If the former had striven without the latter's aid or assistance, it could not, I am persuaded, have held its own against barbarism and anarchy, as it did not hold its own in the ages which immediately preceded the revival of the Pope's authority, during the time which elapsed between the times of Charles the Great and the Norman conquest. The Pope had every reason to be on good terms with these new institutions.

But the English king was also from the same period the centre and instrument of order. He had to struggle against the turbulence and wilfulness of his nobles, and the dangerous independence of the clergy, and he sometimes had to use force, sometimes to invoke law, for furthering his ends. It was his interest, also, to seek allies in the men of the new culture, who, though clerks, were bent upon study, and would, out of their own independent action, aid him in the functions of government. He was, therefore, ready enough to support the Pope's will by his own charters, as his successors did, sometimes to the distaste of Parliament, as at the beginning of Henry IV.'s reign, or with its assent, as at the beginning of Edward IV.'s.

What I have said about these two powers,

and their effect in the university, may be illustrated from the history and conduct of Bishop
Grostête. This personage was the most conspicuous English churchman in the middle of
the thirteenth century. He was the son of a
peasant, probably a serf, who had been sent to
the university of Oxford, which at that time
was without a single college within its borders.
Here he was the most distinguished pupil, and
the most distinguished teacher of the new learning. When he was, comparatively speaking,
an old man, he was appointed Bishop of Lincoln,
in whose see Oxford then was situated. He
continued his affection to the university in
which he had studied and taught. But he
thwarted both Pope and king; the latter, by
exercising a vigorous discipline over the admission of clergymen to preferment; the former,
by attempting to extend the episcopal authority
over the monastic houses, and by flatly refusing
to accept a papal nominee to a benefice in his
diocese. It is clear that he learnt this independence in the university where he had been
so long residing. His spirit cost him the
honours of saintship, which the English would
have conferred on him, but the Pope refused to
confirm.

From the very earliest times the privileges
of the universities have been a protection to
those who have been identified with innovations
in discipline and opinion, either on religious or
on secular subjects. This has been especially
the case with Oxford, though Cambridge has

adopted the tenets of her elder sister, and has occasionally taken a more prominent part in their development.

Historians have noticed that in the very early days of Oxford, the university of Oxford harboured men whose tenets were entirely distasteful to orthodox opinion, and we are told that some of them were expelled and punished shortly after we hear of its existence. Oxford was the place were Wiklif was taught and sheltered. So obstinate was the defence which the university accorded him, that it abandoned him only when its privileges were threatened with extinction, though when the storm was over it harboured and concealed his adherents, to the great disgust of people in authority. It was at Oxford, in the next century, that Pecok, bishop of Chichester, developed those opinions which led to his deprivation.

At the latter end of the same century (the fifteenth), when the second revival of letters reached England, Erasmus, More, and Colet, the patrons of a restored scholarship, made their first essay on the new lines at Oxford, though it must be admitted that Cambridge rapidly rivalled it in progress. The Reformation was strongest at Cambridge a generation or two later; but Cambridge had been long familiar with Lollard opinions, the precursors of the reformed doctrine. The movement known as Puritanism began at Oxford, and was taken up warmly at Cambridge. The reaction under Laud began at Oxford, which remained faithful

to the tenets encouraged by this prelate, while
Cambridge stood on the whole firmly by those
which the Long Parliament represented.

At the beginning of the eighteenth century
the most remarkable religious movement of
modern times began at Oxford, in the teaching
of the brothers Samuel and Charles Wesley and
Whitfield. These soon parted, the Wesleys
founding a Church which has exercised a prodigious influence over English-speaking people,
and Whitfield having been the reviver of
Calvinism. Perhaps no teacher of religious
opinion has had a wider field than Wesley had
even in his own life, and it is probable that no
form of Protestant belief has been so extended
as his has been.

Lastly, in our own days, the so-called Oxford
movement has been exhibited, the effects of
which have been felt throughout Christendom.
Now, I do not criticise any of these revivals, but
it is certain that nothing has contributed more
to the growth of the British citizen than these
periodical developments of religious activity.
One cannot conceive society without religion.
One cannot interpret it without taking into
account the effect which religion has had in
giving it shape and colour. Civilized man can
no more escape from it than he can escape from
consciousness and life, for it is certain that the
best energies of mankind have been derived
from its authority and precepts.

CHAPTER XXII.

THE WORK OF THE UNIVERSITIES IN REFORMS.

As the religious temperament of man has been moulded by the action of these centres of thought, so the greatest activity in secular affairs has been the direct result of academical teaching and training ; and perhaps the advancement of mankind in that balance of all just interests which makes up the harmony of society, and which it would be arrogant indeed to say is perfect at present, owes more to the highest education than it does to any other force. Foolish men who call themselves practical often sneer at what they call academic opinion, but wise men who are practical know what is the weight of wise and judicious reasoning.

It is not easy to discover what was the special influence which able men before the Reformation had on the progress and the making of England. But after that epoch we can distinguish the great names to which this country owes no little of its growth. It may be useful to point out some of these, and to show what their services were in the domain which they made their own.

In the first half of the seventeenth century the two most distinguished men are Bacon, who was taught at Cambridge, and Selden, who owed his training to Oxford. I do not speak of either as lawyers and statesmen, but as men

who have contributed by their writings to that
which makes up the English mind and character.
The first of them shook the old system of
inquiry to its foundations, and was the first
teacher of scientific method.   The nature of the
second was designated by his motto—" Liberty
about all things."   Selden was the greatest
master of legal principles, of the demonstration
of the reasonableness of law, as opposed to
mere legal forms, in his age, and therefore was
the precursor of that system which insists that
law should be constantly adapted to the wants
of civilized society.

Amid the trouble and turmoil of the civil war,
in which he was himself the agent in some of
its bitterest controversies, there was a service
which Milton did which was not appreciated in
his own age, but bore fruit a generation or two
after him.   He was the first person who put on
a right footing the principles on which the press
should be free.   He did this service, too, at a
time when, in spite of the assistance which he
had given to the dominant party, his proposals
were offensive and unpopular.   Milton was bred
at Cambridge, from which university most of
our great poets, who have had an academical
training have proceeded.

Towards the end of the same century, when
the country was ruled by a singularly depraved
government, and seemed likely to fall under a
despotism, when a freethinker was advocating
that despotism in Church and State, an Oxford
thinker and philosopher put out the defence of

toleration. There was no time in which the advocacy of the tenet was more timely, for it seemed as though the rival religions were bent, whoever got the mastery, on extirpating the other. Locke was an Oxford student, and I make no doubt that the comparative gentleness with which the victorious party used its powers at the Revolution was not a little due to the magnanimity which Locke's wise gentleness commended. In this work he was ably seconded by a Cambridge philosopher, the illustrious Newton, who was as wise a public man as he was a profound thinker.

The most eminent person of the eighteenth century owed his training to Oxford. Adam Smith was a Scotchman, who was educated for nearly seven years at Baliol College. In matters of social and political progress, England owes more, I believe, to this man than to any person who has ever written, for Adam Smith took no part whatever in public life. But he has taught statesmen wisdom from his own day to the present time. Had his teaching been accepted earlier, the American people would probably have still been united to England, for he exposed the system which led to the quarrel. The instruction which he gave, and which taught statesmen that the best interests of their own country lay in the prosperity, and not in the misfortunes, of their neighbours, is part of what may be called the gospel of humanity, for it is the extension of the principles of Christianity to the whole human race, in matters where self-interest seems to be sole guide. There is hardly a position in his great work, "The Wealth of Nations," which has not been at the bottom of every social reform which has been effected from that day to this, and which is not suggestive of reforms that are still to be effected in the future.

Another distinguished Oxford man, more eminent in his day than Smith was, and born a few years earlier than he, was Samuel Johnson. The service which Johnson did in his own time, and has done from that time onwards, was to teach men the duty of candour and the benefit of common-sense. Now, both these qualities have their inconsistencies, for candour may be sometimes rudeness, and common-sense may be prejudiced. But Johnson was a man of un-affected piety, of genuine sincerity, of unbounded generosity, of substantial justice, of unshaken courage, and of great learning. We know by accident more about him than about any considerable person of his age, and he is, and will remain, a household name, and an example for the future as he has been for the past.

A generation and a half after these men another eminent Oxford man, who through a long life remained a student, came to the front and exercised an influence which has been greatly beneficent. To Jeremy Bentham we owe more in the reform of the English criminal and civil law than to any other Englishman. He wrote, and by his writing set Romilly and Mackintosh to work.

The criminal law, when he began to denounce it, was, as I have already stated, absolutely atrocious, so atrocious that even juries thought that mercy was a higher duty than obedience to their oath. As the law stood, human life could be taken for trivial offences. There stood a tombstone in my native place, near the chancel door, which stated, and truly stated, that a yeoman had been convicted and hung for some petty matter, and that all the witnesses to the charge had been suborned by some relation, who, if he could get the man out of the way, would succeed to his inheritance. I am almost sorry that the rector of the parish removed the stone, some time after the law, of which the monument made a record, was repealed, because he thought its language would make the people think lightly of the law.

I have quoted these cases not only as an illustration of the good which the higher education has done for the people, in the hands of wise and courageous men, who have been more than abreast of their times, and not only to put to silence the silly cavil which vulgar people are fond of uttering about unpractical thinkers, as though one could measure the worth of knowledge by its immediate acceptance, but to show how men are trained up to do good work for their time and for all time. Of the names I have quoted, Bacon and Bentham were born, the one in the way of uneasy ambition, to which he owed his well-merited disgrace, the other in easy fortune.

But Selden was the son of a village musician, Milton of a London scrivener, Newton and Locke of no influential stock, Johnson of a travelling bookseller, Smith of a Scotch custom-house officer. The best and the most unstained of them owed nothing to birth, much to their training, most to the unfailing energy of their character.

I could, indeed, speak of many more to whom these benefits of an academical training did not come. There is the common property of English civilization, Shakespeare; the common inherit-ance of English religion, Bunyan. These are but types of the cloud of witnesses. But it is certain, too, that no good work ever dies, and that we English people owe our present growth and life to a host of ancestors, whose pedigree is not traced or traceable, but of whose blood we are.

CHAPTER XXIII.

THE EDUCATION OF THE PEOPLE.

THE higher education in England has been con-tinued regularly, but with great depressions as well as exaltations for seven centuries at our universities. The depressions were during the troubles of the fifteenth century, at the epoch of the Reformation, and during the general dead-ness of the eighteenth century. It cannot be denied, and it ought not to be concealed, that whatever may have been the ultimate benefits of the Reformation, and the benefits were great, its early stages, mainly in consequence of the badness of those who were its instruments, very nearly brought about the ruin of the nation.

The Scotch Reformation busied itself early with the education of the people. Coeval or almost coeval with the new system of ecclesiastical government in Scotland was the parish school, which, though associated with what became ultimately the national Church of the Scottish people, was independent in its existence and always aimed at a high standard of teaching. It is difficult to overrate the benefits which this system has conferred on the inhabitants of the Northern Kingdom. It has made the poorest state in Europe one of the most vigorous, enterprising, and opulent.

The English Reformation, unfortunately, did not plant schools in any parish, and did not therefore do anything for the education of the working classes. There was an intention on the part of the government, as I have said already, that the grantees of the abbey lands should devote a part of that which they received to the endowment of schools. But this scheme was very imperfectly carried out. The actual endowment is that which forms the fund from which the so-called English public schools were founded. But the quantity from the beginning was far short of what was requisite for a system of national education, and very speedily the foundations were appropriated by very different persons from those for whom they were originally designed.

As I have already stated, there is good reason to believe that before the Reformation, what we call primary education was much more widely afforded than people think, and there is equally good reason to believe that after the Reformation the quality and the amount of this education greatly deteriorated. It is pretty certain that it became worse instead of better as time went on ; though for an interval, and principally at the epoch of the Protectorate, there was a considerable amount of activity in the direction of education. I draw my inference from the bills sent in by workmen and artificers, thousands of which I have inspected, at various periods of English history.

During the eighteenth century, the education of the masses was as scanty as it was in the darkest ages. I do not believe that a hundred years ago, more than one man in ten, or one woman in twenty, knew how to read and write. Even when they could read the Bible and sign their names, they read with difficulty. When I was a youth in a Hampshire village—where a school had indeed been started by the rector, now sixty years ago, though in many neighbouring parishes there was no school, not even a dame's school—hardly one of the peasantry who was over forty years of age, knew how to read. It was deemed superfluous to give a rudimentary education to the peasant, perhaps even inconvenient.

The movement in education began with the Sunday-school, and it is not easy to détermine whether the clergy of the Established Church, where they had the inclination to carry out such a purpose, or the ministers of the nonconforming bodies when they undertook this duty, are to be credited with the earliest efforts in this direction. It is certain, however, that the duty was performed very irregularly and only in special localities. In course of time, however, this work of individuals was developed into associated work, and active societies were formed by the Church and the Nonconformists almost simultaneously, whose object was that education should be accompanied by religious teaching. Later on State grants, at first very small, were made in aid of schools which satisfied the obligations imposed by the government as conditions of that assistance, and a body of inspectors were appointed, whose duty it was to report on the progress of the school, its scheme of instruction, its discipline, the attendance of the scholars, and the results of the teaching.

It is, however, only fifteen years ago, *i.e.* in 1870, that the machinery of education was supplied to all children, and its acceptance made compulsory. From this time it has become part of the settled policy of this country, that all young people should be educated, and the cost defrayed partly at the public charge, partly by voluntary effort, partly by the payments of parents, partly by grants from the Exchequer. The first two of these resources is a matter of choice. If a locality supplies the requisite funds from subscriptions, the last two sources of income supply what is lacking. If the locality cannot or will not, the initial charges are met by a rate.

The motive which led the State slowly and perhaps reluctantly to undertake the duty of insisting on the education of all, was primarily, and I think justly, an economical one. It was seen that primary education was a means by which other knowledge was imparted more easily and more early. Take the simple case of a soldier learning his drill. It was found that a recruit who had obtained the benefits of education learnt this in half the time, and therefore reached efficiency at half the cost needed for training one who was without the education, and it was reasonably inferred that what applied to one craft, would apply to all, and that consequently education meant a saving of time.

Again, it was observed that in the struggle between nations, other things being equal, the best-educated people would be successful rivals of those who were not so well grounded. Now, within any community, the strife of competition is greatly modified by custom, and by a disposition which most people have, and public opinion commends, of not taking extreme advantage of the position which may have been secured. But in international trade competition is strict and absolute, and success or failure depends entirely on the general effectiveness of industry. Under these circumstances, countries which, being densely peopled, depend largely on their foreign trade for the employment of the people, and indeed for the maintenance of the people, have the highest possible interest in aiding everything which should make labour as effective as possible, and therefore more apt for the struggle of life, and success in the rivalry with other nations.

Certain parts of Germany, especially its northern territories, and the United States, had recognized the wisdom of insisting on a national system of education before the English people had, and in the latter country especially, the establishment of a school is the earliest public duty which a new settlement or town undertakes. There is, indeed, no compulsion in the United States, for no one needs it. The benefits of education are so universally recognized, that all parents send their children to school as a matter of course.

Again, it is felt that education is a great check to criminal propensities. It does not follow that the knowledge itself supplies the check, it may even, as we have too good reason to know, supply the means for more daring or more subtle wickedness, and it is not by any means improbable that the spread of education has suggested fraud in place of violence, cunning in place of daring. Besides, the statistics of crime begin with committals and conclude with convictions. They do not include undiscovered offences, and it is plain that the shrewder and more intelligent an evil-doer becomes, the more does he evade the risk of detection.

But the advantage of education, great though

the value may be of what is taught, chiefly depends on the mode in which the teaching is imparted. The essence of school teaching is discipline, and the discipline must be intelligent, not arbitrary, *i.e.* it is that which the person who is subjected to it sees gradually to be necessary and wise. Now, this discipline is twofold. It implies reasonable obedience to the teacher, and reciprocal good feeling and fairness among the pupils. Children learn that self-will, rudeness, violence, falsehood, evil speaking, are mischievous vices, and to learn that a vice, to which human nature may be prone, brings evil and suffering in its train to the child who yields to it, as well as to those who suffer from it, is a training of incalculable value. Nor does the rivalry and emulation among the scholars bring about bad feeling. Children, and for the matter of that young men, are generally very just to one another, and are free from many of those selfish vices which a more advanced age develops among the struggles of later life.

CHAPTER XXIV.

EDUCATIONAL BRIDGES.

I have dealt with the process by which the more intelligent and well-to-do persons are trained in England, up to the duties and privileges of our citizenship, and how those who never get beyond the labours which must remain the business of

most among us, have at last, and none too soon,
obtained their training.   I do not disparage, I
repeat, the value of what they learn, but incom-
parably more important is the process by which
they learn.   The experience of a well-ordered
and well-conducted school, in which the master
is wise and the pupils are rationally dutiful, is
the best part of all education, and is of incalculable value.   If young people behave well,
they are pretty sure to learn well.

But there is something else which has to be
done, something which was lost in the great
confusion which followed on the Reformation.
Before this time it was common for persons of
very humble, of even what was called low condition, to rise to places of authority, trust, and
dignity.   The theory of the law was that half
the working population should be condemned
to a perpetual disability.   The fact was that
these persons frequently got over what were
supposed to be insurmountable barriers, and
became among the most eminent persons of
their age.   I have already pointed out how the
university, the monastery, and the Church were
agents in this result.

It is plain that if there be a personal right at
all, it is the right that an individual should be
able by honest and innocent efforts to better
himself.   Men are of value by reason of the
service which they do to their fellow-men, and
if hindrances are put on an individual who would
or could do a service, he is wronged, and society
is wronged too, for it has to put up with inferior

services when it might perhaps have had superior ones. Men of all ranks of life have done good to their fellow-men, and character and capacity are not the privilege of any station. It is clear, then, that as these gifts, or graces, or powers may be discoverable in all conditions of men, all men should have an open career, if they have the courage, the skill, and the constancy to take advantage of it.

It is often said that genius will surmount all obstacles. The most wonderful English genius was the son of a poor burgher in a country town, who left his home to follow the despised and degraded calling of a player. The genius of whom our Scotch kindred are justly proud, was the son of a small farmer, whose position in life was hardly higher than that of an English farm labourer. Instances of this kind might be multiplied. But we never can tell what the world has lost by the difficulties which have denied the abilities of others a fair career. I do not say that there could have been a dozen Englishmen like Shakespeare, and a dozen Scotchmen like Burns, but we never can tell whether there might not have been more than one if the chance had been given.

Besides, genius is one thing and usefulness is another. It is true that the highest usefulness is found in well-directed genius, but there are many forms of supreme usefulness which one could never call genius, and there may be many men who could do the work which has to be done, better than those into whose hands it happens to be entrusted. At any rate, such persons should have every opportunity of showing and proving their ability.

In the competition of life, all of us who have any experience of men, though their acquaintance with such matters may be narrow, can point out people who have raised themselves from humble position to wealth and rank. There is a work written by Mr. Smiles, the object of which is to point out how such persons have lived and risen. Self-help, however, though a just end of life, is by no means the highest end ; and perhaps a trifle too much has been said and written about those who get wealth. That man has done best by the generation in which he lives, who has left his mark on his generation by the good which he has done. And what is true of men as individuals is true of institutions.

Now the problem has been : How can a youth of capacity, diligence and character, rise by the machinery of the highest education from the poorest to the best prospects ? The road has never been closed in the ordinary business of life, but a quarter of a century ago there was no opportunity given for a lad such as I have described to rise from the national school to the university, and thence into any walk of life for which his abilities fitted him. At present, the path is fairly open, and I am glad to say that many such persons have been discovered and helped on, as they were helped on in old times, though by a different process.

About thirty years ago, the legislature made

great changes in the constitution of the universities and the colleges of Oxford and Cambridge. Limitations of their endowments to particular localities, schools, and families, were in general swept away, and the endowments were thrown open to all persons, under certain conditions of proficiency, and for a time of conformity. This change gave a strong stimulus to the endowed schools, for while the preferences which existed to most of these schools were greatly modified, such schools as were not specially favoured came into the competition, and, when they were in energetic hands, became well known from being obscure and frequently useless.

At this period the University of Oxford stepped in by its own action. It offered to examine schools, and especially those schools in which the middle classes were taught—schools at that time at a very low condition of efficiency. Oxford was soon followed by Cambridge, and a very efficient system of examination was established. Many grammar schools adopted the scheme, especially those which, having been neglected or mismanaged, were now emulous after a higher reputation. In course of time, some of the Oxford colleges offered the most successful boys in the senior examination advantages or aids to their higher education, and I well remember that one of the first of these aids was given at a distinguished Oxford college to the son of a poor widow, a laundress in South London, and that the young man amply justified the help given him.

But the constitution of the old endowed schools was very defective. They were cramped by regulations made at a time when the future could not be foreseen, and the machinery by which these constitutions could be changed was dilatory and costly. It was therefore determined by Parliament that a commission should be created for the purpose of giving facilities for such salutary changes as would make the schools more efficient, and in some cases should aid them by adding obsolete charities to the school endowment. In this manner, many schools were remodelled, and many are even now being re-modelled. The result has been that intermediate education has been greatly improved, and in general, care has been taken that these newly constituted foundations should, on one side of the school at least, be conformed to the more modern wants of the time in which we live, and the exigencies of business. No one, but those who have had experience of what ruled in past time, could form any conception as to the importance of the change which has been effected.

Then came the General Education Act. The last action of the government in remodelling schools, is to introduce a system under which aids are given to boys from primary schools towards their higher education in grammar schools. The scheme is new, imperfect, and not always judicious. But there are many parts of the country in which the machinery is provided by which a boy of the very humblest origin can gradually move upwards to the highest education, and it is to be hoped that more will be done in the same direction.

These ancient endowments were intended for all classes, for the poor most of all ; not because they were poor, but because they were deserving. The process which gives every one a fair and free field for his abilities, is just and fair. No career should be closed to the deserving, and hereafter the way to such a career may be made more open. It does not follow that it will be easy, for the path is not open to a man because he is of poor parents or humble origin, but because he is competent. Education is the right of all, the highest education of all who can attain to it.

CHAPTER XXV.

THE PRESS.

ABOUT the middle of the fifteenth century, a discovery was made in an ancient city on the Rhine, the Church of which had been founded by an Englishman some eight centuries before. This discovery had not been made by the ancients, and perhaps would not have been made at the time, had it not been for another invention, made more than a century earlier. The first in order of time was the invention of paper, the second was that of printing with movable types.

For twenty or thirty years before printing

was invented, as we now know it, something
like it had been practised.   Blocks of wood had
been engraved with rude drawings and writings,
and these block books as they are called, are
still in existence in public libraries.   But the
peculiarity of the new system was, that the types
were movable.   We do not know what was the
first book which was printed with movable
types, but the first book with a date is a splendid
bible in three volumes, copies of which are
sometimes sold, one a few months ago, for an
enormous sum.   It is as beautiful a specimen
of the printer's skill as anything which is printed
now.   Naturally, it was made to imitate a
manuscript, and so wonderful was the new art,
that the inventors of it were supposed to have
produced their books by magic.

For a long time the new art, when its real
process was discovered, was hailed as a general
benefit.   The most valuable books, ancient and
modern, were printed at a price far below that
at which they could be obtained in manuscript,
and printing presses were set up everywhere.
The ancient monasteries busied themselves
with it, and enterprising men of business set
themselves actively to work in order to satisfy
the growing demand for books.

After men had become familiar with this new
instrument of learning, the great event of the
sixteenth century, the Reformation, occurred,
and a revolt was made against the authority of
the Roman Church.   The printing press was
an essential service to this movement, so great

a service that it does not appear how the new doctrine could have spread or been made accessible without it. The Reformation was not conducted in a very courteous manner, and the authority which was assailed was also insulted. The innovations of the new teachers were displeasing enough, but the warfare was carried on in the plainest, rudest, and most offensive manner.

Now, from very early times, though not from the earliest, the Church had taken upon itself the function of controlling opinion. The old Church encouraged intellectual activity. It was the steady patron of learning ; but it demanded that learning should be submissive to authority, should aid it, not thwart it. It punished those who employed their abilities in criticising it in an adverse or unfriendly spirit. The history of the Christian Church is full of instances of men who were, in the early part of their career, the favourites of those who exercised ecclesiastical authority, but who after a time became the objects of its anger, who were persecuted and punished. It was natural that authority should resent what it thought was an abuse of the new engine of knowledge, and should take any step which it deemed necessary or convenient in order to bring this instrument under control.

But it was not the authority only of the heads of religion which was slighted, or criticised, or lampooned. The ferment and turmoil of the age turned men to the function of criticising the acts of kings and governments. For a long time, indeed, it was not easy to separate affairs of religion from affairs of State; for the party of reformers always strove to get the upper hand in the State for that which they conceived to be right, and therefore the highest duty which government could carry out.

About a century after the Reformation began, the press was employed for the discussion of what may be called secular subjects—the principles of government and law, the rights of prince and people. In one sense the thirty years' war, which desolated Germany, was a religious war, just as the revolt of the Netherlands had been a generation or two before. In another sense it was a political war, in which the authority of the temporal ruler was challenged. Similarly, our great war between king and Parliament was at once a religious and a secular war. This war was carried on not only with armies, but with the weapons of literary controversy.

The hardest and the last lesson which a government learns, is that of bearing criticism on its conduct. The higher it rates its authority, the more impatient it is of any cavilling at its doings. The Parliament professed to be struggling for liberty, but when it got the mastery, it was as eager to punish its critics as that government had been which it conquered and superseded. It was to correct this spirit that Milton wrote the most famous of his prose works—that which claimed the liberty of the press.

The process by which the government

checked the liberty of the press was by subject-
ing all books to the inspection of a licenser,
whose permission was necessary for the publica-
tion of the volume. But it is quite certain that
the precaution was ineffectual, that many un-
licensed pamphlets were printed secretly, and
disseminated secretly, for such pamphlets without
the licence of the authority are found by
hundreds, during the continuance of the censorship, in public libraries.

At last, mainly owing to the utter incom-
petence of the persons who were appointed to
the office, the function of licenser was abolished,
nearly at the end of the seventeenth century.
It seemed to be a dangerous experiment to
allow the freedom, for parties were very bitter,
the settlement of the government seemed anything but secure, and the press kept issuing the
grossest libels and lampoons. But in general
these violent writers did no harm to that which
they assailed, and were of no service to that
which they defended.

In one direction, however, the freedom of the
press was not allowed. It remained for a long
time, for nearly a century, a very grievous
offence for any person to print in pamphlet,
magazine, or newspaper, any account of what
was said or done in either House of Parliament;
and printers were imprisoned and otherwise
punished for contravening by such publications,
what were conceived to be the privileges of
Parliament.

There had once been a reason for this.

When the struggle was going on between the king and his advisers on the one hand, and the members of Parliament, especially those of the House of Commons, on the other, any information given as to the speech or vote of individuals, might be and often had been dangerous to them. Elizabeth frequently imprisoned members who had given her offence, as had also her two immediate successors. It was natural, therefore, that Parliament should cherish the secrecy of its proceedings, as long as the safety of the individual was compromised by the openness of his speech.

As soon, however, as the members of the Houses of Parliament were allowed complete liberty of debate, subject to rules of decency and order, the motive for this secrecy passed away, and the privilege became mischievous, as the public had no means of knowing whether its representatives kept faith with them by speech or vote. It has been pointed out that much of the corruption justly charged on members of both Houses during the eighteenth century, and indeed before it, from the Restoration onwards, was fostered and hidden by this practice.

Macaulay says that the abolition of the censorship was mainly brought about by the intrigues of a thoroughly bad man. The liberty of the press in relation to parliamentary reporting was certainly secured by one of the worst men of the eighteenth century, Wilkes, who successfully defied the House of Commons when they strove to arrest the printers of their debates.

But from this time the proceedings of Parliament are open. The report of what is said there, and the manner in which members vote, is freely published, and in so far as the press is an engine of political education, it is allowed to comment at discretion on the doings and sayings of those public men to whom debate in Parliament and the administration of public affairs is entrusted.

CHAPTER XXVI.

THE ACTION OF THE CLERGY.

In his account of what constitutes the wealth of nations, and of the various powers which unite society together, Adam Smith makes use of a singular expression about the Church, i.e. the clergy, when he ranges the endowments of the clergy under those of such revenues as are devoted to the promotion of education. He describes the clergy as engaged in the education of persons of all ages. He was of course referring to the ministrations of the clergy in his own day; but it would be an imperfect sketch of the history of progress, and the means by which the British citizen has been developed, if we omitted to notice the part which the clergy have played in the making of our people.

It has been justly remarked that in all countries which have a true government, or a true constitution, and a place in the general growth of civilization, there always will be two parties. These have been called the party of progress and the party of order. There are times in which the maintenance of order is so important, that every valuable social force is enlisted on its side ; there are occasions in which progress has been so imperatively urgent, that the most settled friends of order are as eager for it as the most vehement advocates of change are.

Now, in the early history of our race and its civilization, that function in defence of the order of society which the clergy fulfilled was of such supreme value that it is not easy to understand how, had it not possessed activity and authority, society could have emerged from barbarism. The early settlers in England were not, indeed, fierce and untamed savages. They were inferior in civilization to part of that which they super-seded, the relics of the Roman system ; they were superior to part of it, the uncivilized and expelled natives. I have described the society which they formed, its close local ties, its feeble central authority at the best, the incessant wars which were waged between the tribal settlers, and the imperfect submission to which the most vigorous and capable of their kings reduced the settlers.

In course of time they accepted Christianity, far earlier at the extremities of the island than in its centre. The south and east were Chris-tianized generations before the midland counties were, and yet at various periods south and east were overrun by savage pagans, who extirpated, as far as they could, religion from its earliest seats.

Now, Ireland was converted to Christianity at a far earlier date than England was, and it appears that much of Scotland, even in its northern and western parts, was brought under this influence. But for many a long day after order and government had been established in England and southern Scotland, these older seats of Christianity remained a mere chaos, in which there never was peace, much less order.

The cause of the difference is, I think, plainly to be referred to the fact that the Church of the period which preceded the Conquest and followed it for five centuries was an offshoot of the Roman Church, was in close communion and relation with it, was strong as the Roman Church was strong, and weak as that central power was weak. The worst condition of the English Church before the Conquest was in the century which preceded that event. But this was also one of the worst epochs of the Roman Church. The best age of the unreformed Church of England from that even to the Reformation was in the twelfth and thirteenth centuries, when that Church was in its greatest vigour, the worst was in the fifteenth, when the Church of Rome was scandalously corrupt.

It would take far too much space to point out how useful the authority of the papacy was in the history of civilization. Secular authority in the greater part of the western world was barbarous, violent, and destructive. If there had been no power of which it stood in awe, there is and could be no reason why the new inhabitants of western Europe should have made a single step from the condition in which they were when they emerged from the wild forests and plains of the east, and occupied the seats of ancient civilization. But they encountered here a force, with which they treated at first, with which they next associated themselves, to which in various degrees they finally submitted. The submission or deference of those potentates was the first step to genuine progress, and, however it may be criticised now, was a necessary step.

When modern historians write about the submission of Henry to Gregory in the eleventh century, or about the persistent animosity of the Popes to the House of Swabia in the next two centuries, and of the base submission of our king John to the legate of Innocent, they criticise those events in the spirit of the Reformation. But I am pretty sure that at the time in which those events occurred, every one who could interpret what was essential to order and government, would have been more disposed to side with the Pope than with the king. When the influence of this central authority was held to be mischievous or superfluous, it was repudiated; but I am convinced that all acquiescence in authority is due, when such acquiescence is voluntary, to the assurance that it is useful or beneficent.

It is due to the Church of the Middle Ages, that we have the relics of ancient literature preserved to us, that there was a refuge from oppression, a check to tyranny, and an energetic criticism on misgovernment. The people used the authority of the Pope against the king, the king used the same authority against a turbulent aristocracy. In time, to be sure, both monarch and people outgrew the necessity of this aid, but for a time it was of supreme value. Of course I do not say that the influence was never abused. But it was, as I read history, less abused than any other political force.

The Roman Church desired that men should be educated and be at peace. But every authority takes care to protect itself, and naturally, if its authority is disputed or shaken, it will sacrifice the ends which it proposes in order to secure the main end of its own action, its own power. It desired that men should be taught, but that they should be taught only on its own terms. It encouraged mental activity, but it soon required mental submission. It purposed to encourage that which it thought itself at last constrained to persecute.

That which I have said is illustrated by the attitude which two of the best-known prelates of the pre-Reformation period took at critical times in English history.

Becket was the friend and favourite of Henry II. He had been most useful to him in the early reforms of his reign, reforms urgent beyond measure, and requiring a strong hand and watchful eye.   By his help the kingdom was settled, and the royal house firmly seated on the throne. Now, as the king had subdued the rebellious nobles, he resolved on bringing the Church under discipline, and thought that Becket, who was still a layman, would be the best instrument for this end.   Becket saw the facts more clearly than his master did, and told him that if he were made archbishop, he would be forced to resist him, and that their friendship would be at an end.   The king insisted on his compliance, and the sequel of the events is known to all who read English history.   The Pope was in exile, was resisted by an anti-pope, and threatened by the emperor.   But he was too strong for the powerful king of England, as Becket foresaw.

On the other hand, less than fifty years afterwards, the most powerful Pope in history quarrelled with our king John.   He forced the king to accept an archbishop in Langton, and ultimately to surrender his crown.   The Pope, undoubtedly, calculated that Langton would be his willing agent.   But this archbishop was the principal means by which John was forced to sign the Great Charter, and to give guarantees of good government.   When the Pope released him from his obligations, Langton held him to them, and finally got the better of both Pope and king.   The times had changed, and Englishmen had begun to learn how to conduct their own affairs, rudely and roughly I allow, without that foreign interference which had been necessary.

The political power of the Pope in England was practically at an end at the conclusion of the thirteenth century.

CHAPTER XXVII.

THE GROWTH OF TOLERATION.

THERE always was what we should call a national Church in England, *i.e.* a Church which taught that the first business of the subject was to be an Englishman. The men who represented the feeling are found in very unexpected quarters. In the circumstances which preceded the quarrel with Becket, nearly the whole of the bishops sided with the king, in what were supposed to be English interests. In John's reign, the most English of the bishops, as I have said, was the Pope's nominee, Langton. In the reign of John's son, the great Grostête was intensely English in his sympathies, and if in the next century the clergy quarrelled with Wiklif, it was not because he denounced the authority of the Pope, but because he disparaged the Pope's doctrine, a system which they were not as yet prepared to dispute.

When the Reformation came, and the people, except during a short reaction during Mary's reign, finally broke with Rome, the most strenuous opponents of that short reaction were Gardiner and Bonner, both men who are set down as cruel persecutors, while the far more gentle Pole was actively anxious to restore all those relations which had been interrupted by Henry.

After the Reformation the clergy of the Established Church (practically all the clergy, with the exception of a few who still adhered to the old faith, and some sectaries as yet by no means numerous) generally adhered to high views of the royal prerogative and were ready to support, though with different theological views, the government of Elizabeth, and the government of the Stuarts. They and their opponents, the Puritans, were equally anxious to model the Church and control the people to their own ends. The advocate of Whitgift's system, and the advocate of Cartwright's system, would have made no terms with his opponent, but would have forced him to submit if he could have had his way. Both sides were eager for uniformity.

Toleration, in the best sense, *i.e.* a genuine conviction that truth and justice are not served by the violent repression of opinion adverse to our own, even though we accept our own opinion with sincere conviction, is the last and the hardest lesson which civilized man learns. There may be and there has been in times long past, the toleration of contempt. The man who disbelieves everything which others believe, may affect, and has often affected, a negligent pity for those whose convictions he repudiates. This was the toleration expressed by sceptical philosophers towards Christianity in its earlier days.

But genuine toleration, which looks on a different judgment from its own with consideration, is a late growth and a rare growth, though it has made much progress in our own day.

Two or three centuries ago, it could not be accepted. Men had been educated into believing not merely that false opinion, as they held it, was injurious to the man and dishonouring to God, but that it ought to be extirpated, if not by severe punishment, still with permanent disability. When the principles of the Reformation were in the ascendant, the adherents of the old religion were extirpated relentlessly, as in Sweden. When the government adhered to the old faith, the same measure was dealt out to the Protestant. It is said that a large majority of the people in Austria were Lutherans or Calvinists at the beginning of the Thirty Years' War, and that these opinions were nearly extinct at the end of that period. Great part of the south and west of France was Protestant at the end of the sixteenth century, and hardly a fraction was left at the end of the seventeenth. In Scotland at one time the Episcopal party persecuted the Presbyterians, and a generation after the Presbyterians rabbled the Episcopalian clergy.

The principle of Toleration was first introduced into the English statute-book, immediately after the Revolution, in a halting and imperfect way, but with purposes more liberal than the words of the statute implied. It had become necessary as well as just to be tolerant. A

generation before, the dominant sects had persecuted the Episcopal clergy, had ousted them
from their livings, had suppressed their system
of government. When retaliation was possible
it was also natural, and the restored Church
dealt harshly with the sectaries. Had the
Church at the revolution thrown in its lot with
the Stuarts, the same process would in all likelihood have been revived when James was forced
to abdicate.

But for a time at least the clergy of the
Established Church had made common cause
against the king's policy and government with
the other malcontents. They had been harshly
treated, and the Nonconformists had accorded
them their active sympathy. At the stand
made against the Declaration of Indulgence, the
Dissenters had refused to go with the king.
When the trial of the seven bishops took place,
the Nonconformists were as eager for their
defence as Churchmen were, and were as
thankful for their deliverance. After so strong
an evidence of common feeling, it was impossible to perpetuate a mutual enmity.

From that time onward the progress of toleration has been gradual but steady. It was not
easy, to be sure, after the offence had been
given, to show the same generosity to the
adherents of the unreformed faith, and more
than a century and a quarter elapsed before
our Roman Catholic fellow-countrymen were
admitted to equal rights with the rest of
the English people. But even the Noncon-

formist was put under disabilities for the same
period.

It cannot, I think, be said that religious zeal
and sincere conviction, as manifested in its
best way, have been weakened by the acceptance of the principles of toleration.   Since the
Reformation the most intolerant age was that of
Charles II.   It was certainly the most immoral,
one in which outward conformity was coupled
with shameless vice and hardly concealed scep-
ticism.

But it is not in religious opinion only that the
principle of toleration has had so humanizing an
educational value.   It has been extended to
other forms of opinion.   There is as much
division among Englishmen on political topics
as there ever has been on religious grounds.
Men feel warmly, sometimes even angrily, on
public questions, speak strongly and work
vigorously.   But the bitterness of political faction
has passed away.   We cannot hear the prayer
which is appended to the service for the day of
the accession of the sovereign with the same
feeling which they must have had who penned
it.   We are all, the warmest among us, ready
to admit that provided a public man has a just
and honest English interest before him, we
should credit him with fairness and listen to
him with patience.   If we take up a newspaper
of forty years ago, we shall be amazed at the
coarseness and virulence with which rivals spoke
and wrote of each other.   Another generation
back and it was worse still.   The worst motives

were ascribed to men in the pamphlets of the
day, at the very time when the liberty of the
press was conceded.

The same comparative gentleness is shown
in the ordinary business of life. I can remember
the time when the farmers made almost open
war on the clergy. It is not so long since that
trade disputes were settled, or rather embittered,
by atrocious violence and outrage. I can quite
understand the heat with which working-men
used to look on what threatened them not with
loss only, but imperilled their livelihood. But
the conduct which was common a generation
ago is rare now, and is discredited. Disputes,
often lamentable, often disastrous in their results,
are carried on with a patience and a temper
which would not long ago have seemed un-
naturally tame.

This, too, has been accompanied by a tenderness towards distress and suffering which is
perpetually awake. Men do not suffer more
now than they did in past days ; but their suffer-
ings are better known. To my mind the
charities, regular and occasional, of this country,
are the most singular fact in its modern civilization, and the best point of it. Gentleness to the
young, compassion to the sick and weak are
shown, even by men who are otherwise rough
and uncultured. But compassion is no enemy
to justice and fair dealing, for the man who is
educated in generous sympathy for others in
their distress, has by the very process, taught
himself to consider and give due weight to the

rights of others. But such an education has been very slowly imparted, though its development is the most hopeful factor in the moral progress of the English people.

CHAPTER XXVIII.

PUBLIC OPINION.

I HAVE stated, more than once in the preceding pages, that the course of civil and material progress in England has not been continuous, but has been interrupted; that at times very remote the prospects of the English citizen have been brighter than they were at times comparatively recent; and that, in short, the history of his political and social life has not been that of a level course, but has been varied by exaltation and depression. The Englishman was more free and was better off in the fifteenth than he was in the sixteenth century, in the first half of the eighteenth than in the first half of the nineteenth. There have, indeed, been times in which public liberty and the progress of the people seemed to be hanging in the balance, and only what seem to be accidents saved the nation from a decline like that of Spain and Italy.

Now that there must have been something vital but not very visible in the national character, which arrested forces or influences which were unfavourable to its growth, and

even at times perilous to its existence is manifest.
There were people who discerned it from time
to time. The earliest writer on the English
character and constitution is Fortescue, a judge
of the fifteenth century, and an adherent of the
House of Lancaster, whose banishment he
shared. In exile he wrote a book in praise of
the English constitution. It was for the use
of the young prince, the son of Henry VI., who
was slain at Tewkesbury fight in 1471, and was
intended to be a treatise on the art of government for his guidance. The writer emphatically
insists on the superiority of law to the authority
of the sovereign. Even after this writer had
made his peace with the young prince's conqueror, he saw no reason to alter his views on
the limitations put by the very life of the English
constitution on the prerogatives of government.

Henry VIII. was a far more absolute sovereign, in the sense of one whose will was other
men's law, than any king before him or since.
But he and his successors knew that there was
a limit beyond which they could not strain their
authority without serious danger to themselves.
The next family could not be taught by opposition or by reverses this important lesson, and
in consequence their history was full of calamities.

There always has been, in fact, a latent power
in the English people which leads them to
resent the mismanagement of their affairs. It
is remarkable that it has frequently been exhibited at times when it was least expected.
The insurrection of the labourers in 1381 was

as unforeseen as a thunderstorm in a clear
sky. The revolution which led to the deposi-
tion of Richard, in 1399, was equally a surprise.
The House of Lancaster was victorious, and
seemed likely to put an end to the civil war in
the last days of the year 1460. In the spring
of 1461 the hopes of the party were lost. So
in the summer of 1688, there seemed no prospect
that the government of James would be overset.
In the winter of the same year, every one had
deserted him, and his case was hopeless.
Similarly, since in later times we have fortunately exchanged parliamentary elections for
these violent efforts, and have reduced the
criticism of government to a system, people are
constantly surprised at the suddenness with
which, at the crisis of opinion, a change of confidence is expressed by the public. The fact
is, opinions are slowly matured by processes
which are often undiscerned by people who are
supposed to make it their especial business to
watch and be on the look out for what is at hand.

Of course, it is to be expected that they only
who can act through the possible modes of
action will act. It is highly probable that the
law of Henry IV., which declared that the
county franchise belonged to all suitors in the
county court and others, and was therefore
equivalent to all the male inhabitants, declared
after all, only that to be law which had long
been custom. It is clear from what has been
said above (p. 100) that the people found out
that they had a new means of expressing their

opinions, and that they used it to the alarm and
vexation of the majority, and that the concession
or admission was narrowed in future.   It is not
at all unlikely, indeed, that the Lollards, who
were a great but secret power, exercised their
franchise in favour of those who furthered
reforms in Church and State.

The power of law, especially new law, was
very weak, and custom was in great degree law,
as long as law itself was custom.   Now it is
quite certain that for a very long time, the
written law was supposed to be nothing more
than a comment on the unwritten, or as it was
called, the common law.   Hence, whatever was
custom was sacred, and it was a custom, which
some people at the time recognized as an obli-
gatory custom, that men should right grievances
by force.   Against this opinion, strongly but
secretly felt, rulers tried to set up, not only the
laws they enacted, and the powers by which
they strove to give effect to these laws, but
opinions about, for example, the divine right of
kings, the duty of passive obedience, and the
wickedness of resistance even to bad government.   We may depend on it that such opinions
would not have been inculcated in books and
in pulpits, had it not been that there was a
spirit abroad which they wished to check, and
saw that law by itself could not check.   In
these later times men obey the law, and the
authority by which the law is exercised, much
more thoroughly than they did two or three
centuries ago, and therefore they have ceased

to need the propagation of opinions which were intended to assist the law.

This habit of resisting law by force, bad and mischievous as such a practice was, lasted very long, and has had marked effects in modifying law. It is, no doubt, disastrous that law should be modified by the violence of those who refuse to submit to it, or who connive at its breach, but it is none the less true that some of the most important reforms in civil life have been effected by those who have deliberately broken a law which they are convinced is unfair or even ill-advised. Of course the proof of the perfection of law is that frame of mind in the general public which leads them to the conviction that what the law says is the best for them and the best for society. Now in many, very many, particulars, perhaps in most, this is the frame of mind in which the vast majority of Englishmen contemplate the greater part of the legal system under which they live, at least as regards its principles.

The education by which this result has been arrived at is in the highest degree significant. No result is more important in the making of a nation than the formation of a sound public opinion, and on nothing is such an opinion more important than in a loyal acquiescence in the laws under which a nation lives. But the process by which this temper is developed is of the highest value. To have tested one system, to have noted its shortcomings and its excesses, to have altered it. so as to keep what is serviceable in it, and to have rejected what is erroneous or mischief-working, is the worthiest labour that any one can be engaged in, and the happiest result we can achieve.

The last English revolution happened nearly two centuries ago. Since that time the English people has without violence, but occasionally with a great deal of plain speaking, been amending its constitution. Other countries have passed through violent action and violent reaction, and many of them, as we are told, are seething with forces which may at any time explode with violence. The English people has won for itself during the last two centuries reforms in which all agree now, the struggle for which was bitter, and from the issues of which permanent enmities and feuds were expected. It is not too much to say that there never was a time in which political animosity was less bitter, and political rivalry more generous.

CHAPTER XXIX.

PROGRESS UNDER REPRESSION.

In point of fact, progress under a system of repression, and in modern times, under a system which justifies criticism and lawful resistance to established practice, is the most useful process by which the social education of a people may be perfected. It is quite possible to extinguish an opinion. It may be so ruthlessly persecuted

that it is deprived of all vitality, even though
the vitality is the growth of centuries. It may
be disproved so thoroughly that the continual
acceptance of the opinion may make a man
ridiculous. It may be examined so judiciously
that the better parts of the opinion may be ex-
panded and developed into a new principle of infinite value, while the worse parts may be thrown
aside as unworthy of any attention. It is not
difficult to illustrate these positions by details.

I have referred to the insurrection of the serfs
in 1381, and the agencies by which it was
brought about. The struggle for social freedom
was, in the main, led by those who were also
engaged in the struggle for the freedom of
religious opinion, not, it must be remembered
for the freedom of other persons' views, for
there was no theory of toleration at that time,
but for the substitution of a new, or as the
promoters would have said, an ancient creed, in
place of that which had been gradually corrupted.

The opinions held by these sectaries were
exceedingly distasteful to persons in authority.
The interests of the more opulent laity were
supposed to be threatened by the democratic, if
not socialist tone of the new doctrine, and the
interests of the clergy, by the persistent attacks
of the same teaching on the opinions and the
opulence of the hierarchy. Hence State and
Church conspired to quell the common foe, and
for a long time continual and relentless war was
carried on against it, every attempt being made
to discover, silence, and punish the preachers.

The chief seat of these new opinions was the Eastern Counties, especially Norfolk, for a long time the wealthiest county in England. There is plenty of evidence as to the vigour with which the crusade against the sectaries was carried on. But the movement was not crushed. There is little doubt that the Reformation in England was more persistently aided by the tenets of the Norfolk and Suffolk peasants than it was by the teaching and authority of these reformers who took their cue from the State. Repression had not destroyed them, it had only rendered them more acute, more silent, and more active.

In great degree the movement which led to the war of succession in the fifteenth century was an effort after reforms in the administration. Henry VI.—the son of the great warrior who had invaded France, subdued it, and for a time had annexed it—was always a child, pious, even saintly, but incapable of government. As his reign went on the administration of affairs fell into the hands of persons whom the people suspected, distrusted, and finally detested. It is quite clear that the Duke of York, who very likely thought he had a better title to the crown than the reigning king, aimed at nothing more for a time than of displacing the king's bad advisers and ministers, and of strengthening the government by putting better men in their place. But I do not wish to dwell on the causes which led to what are called the Wars of the Roses.

It was chiefly in the Eastern Counties, where the people were strongly predisposed to Wiklif's reformation, that the duke and his associates found supporters, while it was in the west of England that the strength of their opponents chiefly lay.

After the Reformation was begun and the reaction under Mary Tudor was over, which was materially aided by the Norfolk peasants and artisans, who had good reason to be dissatisfied with the conduct of Edward VI.'s guardians, the spirit of resistance to what was believed to be an unlawful exercise of power on the part of government was mainly kept up in the same part of England. When the struggle between king and Parliament began, the chief strength of the latter was in the Eastern Counties, who formed themselves into an association for political ends. Here it was that Cromwell organized his wonderful army, which, whatever may be the opinion that may be formed as to the merits of the struggle, was the most powerful instrument of warfare which has ever been marshalled and employed. The district in England which took the side of the Parliament in the seventeenth century, had almost exactly the same geographical limits as that which took the side of the White Rose in the fifteenth.

It is remarkable, too, that in this region arose the first sect which openly avowed the principle of toleration. It is not to be expected that any established power, whether it be secular or religious, should voluntarily abandon its authority over the conduct of men; and it is not

N

just to censure such powers for not taking the initiative in such action, however wise it may be in the end. You may search in vain for any national Church, or for the matter of that any national government, which has ever taken the first step in acknowledging any right on the side of those who resist or even criticise it. If this phenomenon has never been exhibited we must find the origin of the existing practice in the general characteristics of human nature. And, as I have stated, the various Church reformers who up to comparatively recent times have quarrelled with the existing order of things, have never pretended any consideration for those whom they wished to supplant and remodel. This was the motive with the Puritan, the Presbyterian, and the Restored Churchman of 1660.

The doctrine that it was not the business of the State, in its religious aspect, to meddle with the opinions of those who dissented from its teaching or discipline was first taught by the Independents or Congregationalists, and was fundamental to their system. But this doctrine and these sects were strongest from the first in the old haunts of the Wiklif movement, in the Eastern Counties of England, and was an entirely spontaneous growth.

There is a repression which has, in the history of English opinion and in the growth of the English character, materially strengthened its fibre and given vigour to its development. To the stand made for the political liberties of

England and for the freedom of private judgment in matters innocent, is in reality due the vigour with which they have been asserted, affirmed, maintained, and secured. We are heirs to a thousand traditions from the times of the Great Charter to the latest victories of popular liberty and social justice. The struggle could not have taken place without resistance, the resistance was sure to take the form of repression, the repression has always been ineffectual ; but the character of the people has grown with the effort it has made and the success it has achieved.

For generations the nation and its leaders withstood the arbitrary government which some of our kings tried to establish or continue. They have been in the end victorious, and have overcome all obstacles. But the loyalty to the political institutions of the country has not been shaken by the resistance which the people has exhibited to some of those who have borne rule. It is, I think, justly alleged that the attachment of the English to the present royal house is far more deep and far more reasonable than it has been to any one of the families which have reigned during past times in the country, and compares favourably with the feeling which is entertained elsewhere. The cause of order has not suffered by the growth of popular liberty.

Again, the disabilities which attached to those who dissented from the discipline and doctrine of the national Church have been swept away. In other countries this toleration, or rather equality, has been followed by fierce onslaughts

on Christianity itself, and the establishment of
political parties whose very essence is the nega-
tion of all religious belief. This has not occurred
with us. The change which has been consum-
mated almost within modern experience has not
been accompanied in England by any such
result ; but on the contrary, there never was,
I believe, a time when the religious sense was
more active, more generous, more considerate,
and less aggressive.

CHAPTER XXX.

COLONIAL ENGLAND.

ONE of the most instructive facts in the narrative
of national progress, is the success with which
the English nation has overcome obstacles to
its development and growth. Its present position is wholly without parallel in history. It
has made conquests like other peoples, but it
may be doubted, or at least it has been doubted,
whether these conquests are a source of strength,
or whether a reasonable estimate of them would
not detect that they are a cause of weakness.
At any rate, any conquering nation of which we
can read has invariably been unable to maintain
for a very prolonged period the effort which it
has made to rule over others. But the case is
very different with the colonies which the nation
and not the government has planted. They are
spread over the whole world. The English

people has settled North America, and the vast
islands of Australasia.   Its government was by
no means wise at first, when it undertook to
deal with the descendants of the English race.

England has undoubtedly great natural advantages.   Its climate is the most equable in
the world, at least in that part of the world
which is neither intolerably hot nor intolerably
cold.   It is situated in that part of the globe
which, being surrounded by sea, and always
accessible, has the largest area inhabited by
civilized societies near its sea board, and it has
the largest variety of natural material, or physical
agents of industry within accessible distance.   It
is better situated for manufacture and commerce
than any other part of the globe, and for both
of these in the greatest variety and of the
highest quality.   These advantages have, however, been discovered and secured only after
considerable labour and after serious obstacles
have been surmounted ; for the progress of
England was very slow, and her success was
acknowledged long after that of those who were
earlier in the field.   I do not say that she
profited by the failure of others, but she was
certainly able to avoid some of the errors into
which her neighbours and rivals fell.

England had no part in the discovery of the
sea passage to India, for that was the work of
the Portuguese.   She had little in the discovery
of the New World, for that was mainly the
work of the Spaniards.   When Spain exhausted
herself by conquest, she did not succeed to her

power in the east, for this fell to the Dutch. The principal acquisitions of England for a long time were her colonies in the New World, which were settled in a country the soil of which was exceedingly poor, the climate of which was marked by singular extremes, and the original inhabitants of which were vigorous, wily, and ferocious savages. The colonists were men who fled from persecution, and some of them did not learn generosity from the troubles through which they had gone. Never, I believe, in the history of mankind, were colonies founded, of which the early struggles were more arduous. In time they have grown into the great American Republic, and probably before many generations are over, this republic will contain the largest number of persons living under one government and constitution in the world.

The colonization of Australasia began a century and a half after that of North America. It was not the action of government, but of private enterprise, for the English government has never colonized, except with convicts, and .the free settlers soon resented that practice. It is very likely that much which these settlers did was harsh, cruel, indefensible. They came upon races which were wholly unable to make progress by themselves, or to assimilate with the civilization which they witnessed, but who became mischievous neighbours. It has been seen over and over again that races which cannot be civilized fade away when they come in contact with the more vigorous neighbours of their life, though they may struggle against the process. The ancient inhabitants of Newfoundland and of Tasmania have perished utterly. The native New Zealander is rapidly passing away, though he has been able to learn many of the practices of civilized life.

The English people in these colonies of private adventure, which have gradually adopted the system of English public life and government, have thriven exceedingly and rapidly. But these colonies are unlike anything in history, except those of ancient fame. The career of these latter was remarkably brilliant, and almost uniformly prosperous, though they had a short existence, owing entirely to the fact that the Greeks were never able to devise a national and representative government, but always halted at the stage of a single settlement. Governments have established trading factories and military colonies, but they have never been able to make stable settlements.

The fact is, human communities are never created by authority. Nations may make military conquests, and may hold them long. But the true colony is a voluntary settlement. The settlement grows with more or less rapidity, according to its opportunities. In course of time it necessarily reaches the boundary of a neighbouring settlement, and federation with its neighbours becomes a practical and soon an inevitable problem, which it is bound to solve, and does solve in one way only.

That an Englishman, who takes account of

his place among other peoples, should feel strong in the growth of his race and in its diffusion, by its own inherent vigour, over a vast and ever-increasing area of the world, is perfectly natural. But he should be also aware that he has done this by his own energy, and by the beneficent abstinence of government from the pretence of directing him. Attempts were made by the home government to assert its right over the new country which the settler occupied, and to reserve the soil to the crown, which means the state. These schemes have been wisely abandoned, and the colony is properly made the lord of the land. Nor has the English government committed for a century, the fatal error which alienated the American plantations. It has freely allowed to its colonial offspring privileges and powers which it has long withheld from its people at home. It has even patiently permitted, from time to time, its colonies to virtually lay, at their pleasure, the cost of extension and defence on the mother country, to levy taxes on the English people without their consent. Twenty years ago, nearly half the British army was in the British colonies, at the expense of the British nation, and engaged in adding directly and indirectly to the wealth of thriving colonists. At the present time the expenditure of British capital, voluntarily advanced, we must admit, to the colonies has been so enormous, that nearly all the public works of these settlements have been constructed by it. The payment of interest on this vast sum secures to this country a perpetual excess of imports over exports, and explains in part why it is that in foreign trade, England seems to sell so little in comparison with what she buys.

Into these colonies of the English race there is annually poured the overplus of the English people. Long habit, the comparative opportunity of ready prosperity, the existence of a government whose machinery is easily comprehended, but above all, cheapness of transit and proximity have induced the great number of Englishmen who leave their native land to choose the American republic as the place of their new settlement. But many also go to those other colonies of voluntary origin which are settled in the Southern Seas. It is rare for them to settle in colonies of conquest, and we may be pretty sure, judging from the impulses of Englishmen, that the attempts of other nations to form government colonies will end in conspicuous failure, and therefore need excite no alarm.

At the present time, the Englishman who would push his fortunes in another country can find numerous communities, of the same blood in the main with his own, with the same laws and institutions, planted in the most desirable parts of the world, and ready to welcome him and his labours. He enters, at the moment that he puts his foot on the shores of these settlements, into all the privileges and rights of those who have long sojourned there. The colonist in our free colonies is an Englishman still. He has abandoned no old nationality, he has entered on no new one. I cannot recall to memory, out of all past history, any position which has been so favourable to enterprise as this is, any career which might be so easy and so large.

The wonder is that more Englishmen do not avail themselves of these wide opportunities, and that the crowded industries of our country do not seek these natural means of relief. As it is, many, perhaps the best and most active of our people, to whom the prospect of future advancement by labour and energy is attractive, do resort to these new regions. The free colonies of the English people are the most valuable and the most enduring of its acquisitions, and they possess other qualities because they owe their existence to the spontaneous action of the nation, and are not tainted by a violent origin.

CHAPTER XXXI.

THE RIGHT OF ASSOCIATION FOR PRIVATE AND PUBLIC OBJECTS.

THE most notable fact in the modern life of the Englishman, is the liberty of association which he enjoys. It is in many particulars a very recent concession. Of course, from very early times partnership in business was allowed; in equally early times trading companies were chartered, and often gifted with great powers; in more recent times companies for foreign trade were created and endowed with considerable privileges and monopolies. But this is not the freedom of association of which I am thinking. I am referring to associations for private ends, ostensibly innocent, though it may be distasteful to those who conceive themselves the objects of such combinations.

For nearly five centuries the law was very severe against combinations of workmen entered into with the view of bettering wages. For nearly half this time it appears that the law was unsuccessful in its effort to put down these associations. But for the other half it was. At last, in 1824, the whole of this repressive legislation was swept away, and associations of labourers were tacitly legalized. Of course, the concession was not intended to justify violent action, but only to permit peaceable proceedings on the part of those who joined these combinations. The law will not and should not permit force, and ought to protect those who are made the objects of force.

Up to the same, or nearly the same period, the English law looked with the greatest jealousy and suspicion on political associations. Towards the close of the last century, a society was formed to which several of the peers belonged, the object of which was to bring about Parliamentary Reform. It is probable that the promoters of this movement were incautious in their admiration of the French Revolution, the

conduct of which was at the time comparatively
gentle, though the very first year of it was
marked by terrible excesses.   Even after the
worst acts of the French Revolution had been
committed, there were many Englishmen who
thought that these acts were the consequence
of foolish and unwise intermeddling in the affairs
of France, and that if the people of that country
had been left alone, the excitement would have
rapidly exhausted itself.

But the government of the time was seriously
alarmed at what they conceived to be involved
in these associations, and appointed a committee
of secrecy, who recommended the suppression
of the Habeas Corpus Act, and the prosecution
of those who were the leaders of the movement.
These persons were imprisoned, tried, and acquitted.   There is no reason to believe that
they meditated any mischievous design whatever.   One of them was, to the end of his life,
so profoundly attached to the constitution in
Church and State, that in our day he would be
considered a person of very pronounced conservative opinions.

Foreign countries even now which profess to
have very free institutions, are very suspicious
of any associations and combinations which are
not immediately recognized by government.
Where the government is more or less despotic,
the policy of the State is to forbid and repress
such combinations.   The consequence is that
the countries in which energetic efforts are made
to suppress concerted action swarm with secret

societies, which constantly avow the most
dangerous purposes, and sometimes commit the
most atrocious crimes. The remedy adopted
is not merely the punishment of offenders
against the law, which is reasonable and just,
but more strict repression and more severe
control, with the result of exciting more bitter
resentment.

Sometimes a government tries to meet unwise and unjust demands half way by conceding
a part at least of what these persons require
Now it is a very dangerous thing for a government or a legislature to undertake such changes,
because, apart from the wrong it is doing, it is
going beyond its proper province, which is to
see that right is done to all, and wrong is forbidden and checked. For if it is once supposed that government intends to undertake the
shaping of a citizen's life for him, and lay down
the rules by which he is to seek his fortunes or
earn his bread, it makes itself responsible for
his failure. Three fourths of the social difficulties in which foreign governments find themselves have arisen from the practice of over-
governing their subjects in matters where it is
far better that individuals should find out their
own path or career for themselves.

Fortunately, for more than half a century, the
English government has abandoned all inter-
ference with the liberty of innocent associations.
The consequence has been that not only is the
English people almost entirely untainted with
theories of communism, and still less disposed

to vindicate rights, as they conceive them, by violence, but they have learnt thoroughly that honest and fair self-help is the only legitimate means which should be adopted by persons who try to better themselves, either as individuals or in concert.

Many associations have been formed in England during the last fifty years, the purposes of which have been very adversely criticised, which have failed or succeeded. But hardly any of these, in the course of its career, has been marked by violence. English people are familiar with debates on every conceivable subject, and generally debate with moderation and fairness, even when they are not convinced. The freedom of the press has been followed by temperate action on the part of the press, the freedom of public meeting and association has been used temperately, and violence is universally disclaimed and condemned.

It is quite possible that people may combine or associate together for ends which could be, if achieved, disastrous or mischievous. But as long as they speak out and keep the peace, they may be criticised, and if the opinion of the public is hostile to them, will be criticised. If people in power try to prevent the utterances of such persons, they are apt to give the impression that the advocates of the new opinions are desiring what is right and just, and that they who seek to coerce them have an advantage which cannot be defended, and should be taken away. It is, therefore, the wisdom of government to allow the freest vent to opinion, and to leave its merits to be settled by debate. There is no reason to fear that in this country the acts of legislation will be too rapid, and that the acceptance of a conclusion which has all the appearance of popularity will be premature.

Perfect freedom of speech and opinion is the most conservative force which society can employ. In the first place, many men are content with the protest which the utterance of their opinions implies, and having made the utterance, will not seek the means by which such an opinion can be made a matter of practical action. In the next place, the agency by which opinion is moulded into law or practice is very slow. In the third the energy by which change is effected is so rare, that in most cases it has to be assisted by some extraordinary or unforeseen event. There is hardly a fundamental change in English institutions or practice which has formed an exception to this rule of difficulty, and the difficulty is enhanced the more freely discussion and preliminary action on the subject is allowed and encouraged. If it is the privilege of a British citizen to promote reforms, it is equally his privilege to resist and delay them.

If one examines all the great changes which have been effected by Parliament in the constitution, the social habits, the trade, the administration of law, or the power of interests in this country, it will be found that the progress of opinion in Parliament is as slow, and as much the effect of effort, as it is in the mind of the public.

It generally makes its appearance in Parliament for the first time on the motion of some private member. It is rejected at first by a large majority. It is repeated and the majority diminishes. It finally gets a majority. It is then, generally still on the motion of a private member, and those who go with him, introduced as a bill. Here it has to encounter great risks, and if it succumbs to one of these risks, it is lost for a year. Parliament watches opinion outside them very closely, the press, public meetings, petitions, and wisely enough will not change till the matter is fully discussed outside. No person can carry any bill which the government of the day does not support, and if he be really desirous to get what he wants, he wishes that the government should take the matter out of his hands. A generation often passes between the inception of a change and its completion.

THE END.

PRINTED BY WILLIAM CLOWES AND SONS, LIMITED, LONDON AND BECCLES.

PUBLICATIONS

OF THE

SOCIETY FOR PROMOTING CHRISTIAN KNOWLEDGE.

Most of these Works may be had in Ornamental Bindings,
with Gilt Edges, at a small extra charge.

1. 12. 84.]   [Crown 8vo.

s. d.

Captain Jewell's Wife. By the Author of "Our Valley." With Three page Woodcuts. Crown 8vo. ...*Cloth boards* 2 0

Carl Forrest's Faith. By MARY LINSKILL. With Three full-page Woodcuts. Crown 8vo. ....*Cloth boards* 1 6

Cuthbert Conningsby : A Sequel to "Maud King-LAKE'S COLLECT." By EVELYN E. GREEN. With Three page Woodcuts. Crown 8vo. ....*Cloth boards* 1 6

Crab Court. By M. SEELEY. With Three page Woodcuts. Crown 8vo. ....*Cloth boards* 1 6

Dick Darlington, at Home and Abroad. By A. H. ENGELBACH, Author of "Juanita," &c. With Three full-page Illustrations on toned paper. Crown 8vo. ....*Cloth boards* 2 0

Dresden Romance (A). By LAURA M. LANE. With Four page Woodcuts. Crown 8vo. ....*Cloth boards* 2 6

Good Copy (A) and Other Stories. By F. B. HARRISON. With Three page Woodcuts. Crown 8vo. *Cloth bds* 1 6

Great Captain (The) : An Eventful Chapter in SPANISH HISTORY. By ULICK R. BURKE, M.A. With Two full-page Illustrations on toned paper. Crown 8vo. ...*Cloth boards* 2 0

Griffinhoof. By CRONA TEMPLE. With Four page Woodcuts. Crown 8vo. ....*Cloth boards* 3 6

Hide and Seek : A Story of the New Forest in 1647. By Mrs. FRANK COOPER. With Three full-page Illustrations on toned paper. Crown 8vo............................*Cloth boards* 2 0

His First Offence : A True Tale of City Life. By RUTH LAMB, Author of "The Carpenter's Family," &c. With Three full-page Woodcuts. Crown 8vo. ....*Cloth boards* 1 6

Home and School : A Sequel to "the Snowball SOCIETY." By M. BRAMSTON. With Three full-page Woodcuts. Crown 8vo. .. ..*Cloth boards* 2 6

In His Courts. By MARGARET E. HAYES. With Three page Woodcuts. Crown 8vo. ....*Cloth boards* 2 6

s. d.

Isabeau's Hero: A Story of the Revolt of the CEVENNES. By ESMÈ STUART, Author of "Mimi," &c. With Four full-page Woodcuts. Crown 8vo. ....*Cloth boards* 3 6

Lapsed, not Lost: A Story of Roman Carthage. By the Author of "The Chronicles of the Schönberg-Cotta Family," &c. Crown 8vo. ....*Cloth boards* 2 6

Lettice. By Mrs. MOLESWORTH, Author of "Carrots." With Three page Woodcuts. Crown 8vo. ....*Cloth boards* 2 0

Magic Flute (The). By MARY LINSKILL. With Four page Woodcuts. Crown 8vo. ....*Cloth boards* 3 0

Miles Lambert's Three Chances. By MARY E. PALGRAVE. With Three page Woodcuts. Crown 8vo. *Cloth bds.* 1 6

Miscellanies of Animal Life. By ELIZABETH SPOONER. With Illustrations. Post 8vo. ....*Cloth boards* 2 0

Muriel's Two Crosses; or, The Cross she rejected AND THE CROSS SHE CHOSE. By ANNETTE LYSTER. With Four page Woodcuts. Crown 8vo. ....*Cloth boards* 3 0

Mutiny on the Albatross (The). By F. F. MOORE. With Four page Woodcuts. Crown 8vo...................*Cloth boards* 3 6

No Beauty. By H. L. CHILDE-PEMBERTON. With Three page Woodcuts. Crown 8vo. ....*Cloth boards* 2 6

Not in Vain. By MARY E. PALGRAVE. With Three page Woodcuts. Crown 8vo. ....*Cloth boards* 2 6

One Army (The). By S. M. SITWELL. With Three page Woodcuts. Crown 8vo...............................*Cloth boards* 2 0

Out of the Shadows. By CRONA TEMPLE, Author of "Her Father's Inheritance," &c. With Three full-page Woodcuts. Crown 8vo. ....*Cloth boards* 2 0

Paths in the Great Waters. A Tale wherein is comprised a record of Virginia's early troubles, together with the true history of the Bermudas or Somers Islands. By the Rev. E. N. HOARE. With Four full-page Woodcuts. Crown 8vo. *Cloth boards* 3 0

s. d.

Pirates' Creek (The).   A Story of Treasure-quest.
By S. W. SADLER, R.N., Author of "Slavers and Cruisers," &c.
With Four full-page Woodcuts.   Crown 8vo. ....*Cloth boards*   3   0

Pride of the Village (The).   By A. EUBULE EVANS.
With Three page Woodcuts.   Crown 8vo. ....*Cloth boards*   2   6

Prisoner's Daughter (The): A Story of 1758.   By
ESMÈ STUART.   With Four page Woodcuts.   Crown 8vo.
Cloth boards   3   6

Shadow and Shine.   By MARY DAVISON, Author of
"Lucile."   With Three page Woodcuts.   Crown 8vo.   *Cloth bds.*   1   6

Sketches of Our Life at Sarawak.   By HARRIETTE
McDOUGALL.   With Map and Four full-page Woodcuts.   Crown
8vo...*Cloth boards*   2   6

Three Sixteenth-Century Sketches.   By SARAH
BROOK.   With Three page Woodcuts.   Crown 8vo.   *Cloth boards*   2   6

Turbulent Town (A); Or, the Story of the Arteveldts.
By the Rev. E. N. HOARE.   With Four page Woodcuts.
Crown 8vo. ....*Cloth boards*   3   0

Una Crichton.   By the Author of "Our Valley," &c.
With Four full-page Woodcuts.   Crown 8vo............ *Cloth boards*   3   6

Valley of Baca (The).   By the Author of "Douglas
Deane," &c.   With Three page Woodcuts.   Crown 8vo.   *Cloth bds*   1   6

Wild Goose Chase (A).   By F. S. POTTER.   With
Three page Woodcuts.   Crown 8vo.   ....*Cloth boards*   1   6

LONDON :
NORTHUMBERLAND AVENUE, CHARING CROSS, W.C.;
43, QUEEN VICTORIA STREET, E.C. ;   26, ST. GEORGE'S PLACE, S.W.
BRIGHTON: 135, NORTH STREET.